THE CASE OF THE LAMBENT LAMA

A MORDECAI MACCABBEE MYSTERY

By Alexandra Schiller

Published by
Bookstand Publishing
Morgan Hill, CA 95037
3149_4

The narration contained herein is entirely fictional; any resemblance
to person(s) living or deceased is purely coincidental.

Portrait photography: Perry Davis
Cover design: Alexandra Schiller
Edited by: Eileen Gunther

Special thanks to Jordi Lindegren at the Coquille Public Library for
her research assistance.

ISBN 978-1-58909-740-7

Library of Congress Catalogue #2009655118

Printed in the United States of America

www.bookstandpublishing.com

This book is dedicated to you, dear reader:
May you, and all beings, be free of suffering
and the cause of suffering.

THE LAMBENT
LAMA

PROLOGUE

Deep red, Mandarin-stylized lettering a foot high spread across the two bayed windows and glass-paned door of the little shop on the corner of Glister and Pine Streets:

ORIENTAL IMPORTS EMPORIUM

Facing this store, one would see the window to the left (which bore the word ORIENTAL) dressed with a broad scattering of colorful, paper parasols in various sizes; a neat row of half a dozen pairs of embroidered sateen slippers in equally eye-catching hues; and several cellophane bags containing fortune cookies, long-past their "use by" date, heaped into the corner where the glass slanted inward toward the door. Anyone seeking to recognize a theme or message in the random -- yet clean and dust free -- display would be frustrated, or, at least, disappointed.

Messages are found, however, taped upon the inward slanting windowpanes on both sides of the door. Informing of meetings, activities and up-coming events, most of these flyers -- some printed, some handwritten -- sported Chinese characters as well as English words.

1

Contents in the bayed window to one's right (bearing the word EMPORIUM) were concealed by a beige velveteen cafe curtain hanging across the full width of the window to a height which allowed a couple of feet or so of eastern sunlight -- such as there might be in a morning -- to enter the shop. Behind the curtain, the wide sill space was utilized for ongoing but temporary storage of unopened shipments, emptied cartons and a black metal file box housing 4" x 6" index cards -- draconian maintenance records of Accounts Receivable, Accounts Payable, receipts and pending orders.

Approaching the entrance, one must pull open a screen door before accessing the main door (lettered IMPORTS), pushing it forward and stepping into the incense-fragranced market. It is not burning incense that perfumes the air, but the presence of the heavily scented sticks and cones during shipment together with permeable items that inevitably absorb and perpetuate the off-gassing of myriad fragrances. The unavoidable saturation permeates, in turn, the very air, and caresses -- or assaults, perhaps -- defenseless nostrils.

A large scroll, a Chinese brush stroke rendering hanging on the far wall opposite the entrance, immediately catches the eye: A snow-capped, craggy mountain peak; a delicate mass of evergreen trees spiraling below the snowline are parted at the base of the mountain by a stone-bordered path; a male figure garbed in traditional Oriental vestment is seated on a small boulder; nearby, another leans against a carved walking-stick. Beneath the painting, monthly tear off pages of a current year's calendar are attached, accurately exposing February.

Two commercial, shelved, display units placed parallel with the window stand to one's left, separated from the window, each other, and the back wall by three aisles. Row above row, an appetite-challenging selection of enticing food items rest upon the shelves: packages of chow mein, nanke seimen, udon, bean thread and many other noodle varieties; Jasmine white rice in ten and 20 pound cotton sacks; cans of water chestnuts, chop suey, bamboo shoots, miso soup, coconut milk; small, transparent bags of dried goji berries; boxes of corn starch, granulated and rock sugar, bouillon cubes, sesame seeds, dried black mushrooms; jars of coconut butter, bean paste, gluten, sweet and sour sauce, plum sauce, wasabi and tahini; mind-boggling assortment of bottled soy sauce, vinegar, sesame and peanut oils, saki, sweet rice and plum wines; and, of course, the ubiquitous fortune cookies in bags and boxes...so many delicacies foreign to the Western diet -- and to Kublai Khan's chef, as well.

Along the back wall, left of the art calendar, are found, from floor almost to ceiling, shelves offering chrysanthemum flower and a multitude of other Oriental and Asian tea varieties; bins of dried herbs and spices; and bottles of traditional Chinese medicinal compounds and nutritional supplements.

Passing these and turning left, the shopper discovers the south wall ledges containing dry goods: flip-flop zori sandals, unisex sateen happy coats, and cotton Mandarin-collared jackets with frog fastenings, bolts of silk fabric -- some brocaded -- for purchase by the yard, and cashmere sweaters in a veritable rainbow of hues; kits for creating Origami forms, calligraphy pens and style-sample books, brush-stroke pigment and brushes bundled together inside felt squares and tied with narrow ribbon; and sets of Go, Dominoes, and Mah Jongg games.

Statuettes of Buddha cast in bronze, brass, glass, plastic or porcelain are here, available in whatever size one might desire, arrayed around a tray of carved cinnabar bangle bracelets, necklaces and earrings; ceramic bowls and the deep spoons designed for dipping soup from them, tea pots, cups and saucers; chopsticks of wood or plastic; boxes of incense and a variety of burners for same are logically placed next to candies, candle holders and joss sticks. Bamboo wind chimes, lacking a breeze, suspend eerily motionless and silent.

Returning to the back, west, wall and passing again the medicinals and calendar, one finds a huge, antique, teakwood cabinet; locked, but its glass-paned doors allow viewers the opportunity to admire the collection of ancient Chinese objets d'art within -- the value of each piece determinable only by a knowledgeable art appraiser, and, perhaps, by Madame and Ben Wu. But none of the cabinet's contents are for sale.

Ben Wu's grandfather, who, with two brothers, had come from China to find employment with the booming railroad construction, soon recognized a need among the growing Oriental population for a source of familiar commodities. With savings from his railroad income, he established the Oriental Imports Emporium. He sent for a mail-order bride from his homeland; Ben's father was their only son. A few decades ago, Ben inherited the business when his father died, and continued, with his American-born Chinese wife, to occupy the tiny, two-bedroom flat above the market.

Most of the family heirlooms in the teakwood curio cabinet had arrived here with Ben's grandmother.

In front of the cabinet and about five feet away from the wall is a long, rectangular table bearing open cartons of fresh fruit and vegetables; not as wide a selection now, in winter, as in late summer, when even the shelf beneath the table top overflows with abundant fresh produce. Now, a few cabbage and mushroom varieties, onions, ginger root, horseradish, and garlic buds constitute the seasonal choices. The Oriental Imports Emporium was, in summer months, the only local source for loquats, kumquats, liche, and mung bean sprouts, most trucked from Southern California farms.

Beyond the end of the produce table, cut into the north wall, is the exit into an alley where a steel stairway against the wall's exterior side provides access to the tiny, second-floor living quarters of proprietors Madame and Ben Wu.

Side by side against the remaining width of the north wall interior, a refrigerator and freezer hold meal necessities such as frozen snow peas, spring rolls, shrimp and haki, won ton wraps, bean curd and tempeh; black bean filled dumplings ready to cook, pickled chicken feet, sushi, pickled cabbage and a variety of dim sum -- "those which touch the heart". Beside cans of best-selling soda pop brands there are chilled bottles of goji berry, mango-pineapple and other fruit juice beverages.

The Oriental Imports Emporium does not sell alcoholic drinks, nor tobacco products of any kind.

Projecting from the east wall, an L-shaped checkout counter is next to the main entrance. Beyond this counter, an airline's promotional poster dominates the narrow wall space at the end of the freezer unit and suggests travel to China: white painted faces with dour expressions typical of Chinese opera characters, a pyramid of exotically costumed acrobats, a few ancient terracotta soldiers, and the Great Wall looming in the background.

Focusing again at closer range, one notices a conspicuously outdated manual cash register placed at the corner where the counter sections meet. At the end of a counter, a rotatable rack tempts patrons with small cellophane bags of roasted sunflower seeds and li hing mui, the mouth puckering, dried and salted fruit introduced by 19th century Chinese laborers who carried supplies of the tangy crack seeds on their long voyage across the Pacific Ocean, and is still a favorite snack.

And behind the counter is Madame Wu herself, lying cold and dead on the floor.

MONDAY

Rising taller than most of the mature conifers surrounding its edifice, the stupa's stately gold-capped turret gleamed brilliantly in the winter morning's soft sunlight.

Mordecai Maccabbee took one last, long look at it before gently backing his forest green 1954 MG TF from the spot in the guest parking lot -- a meadow clearing at the opposite end of the monastery grounds and almost a mile from the stupa -- where he had left it three days ago.

"So, was the weekend all you had expected it to be?" Morrie addressed his companion, Pei Jiangiyn, riding beside him in the passenger seat.

"No expectations!" Pei reminded, draping a green cashmere scarf over her head and around her neck. Her fingernails, painted to match her lip color, flashed scarlet with every movement of her hands.

"Oh, right; having an expectation is a set-up for disappointment," he recited, readjusting his grey tweed driver's cap atop his head of black, curly hair. "Well, then, did you enjoy the sessions?"

"Yeh-yeh. Always good to be near Lama Trisong," she replied, making space for her booted feet on the car floor between her overnight case and tote bag.

Morrie guided the vintage roadster's wheels at snail pace down the driveway. It would be at least 15 minutes of gravel crunching before they reached the paved, county road that led to the interstate highway.

"It's a colorful place," Morrie commented, recalling bright, gilt-edged banners flying from posts bordering both sides of the path approaching the magnificent white stupa with its trim of geometric patterns in gold, blue, red, green and turquoise; and cheerful prayer flags flying from lines strung between lecture hall and gift shop, as well as between dormitories.

"Was the women's dorm comfortable?" Morrie inquired, remembering the lack of heat in the men's bunkhouse.

"Yeh-yeh. Not many come here this time of year, I think."

"Well, it is cold!"

"Not as cold as Mongolia, or North China," Pei stated.

"Everything is relative," Morrie mumbled, certain that he did not want to find himself in any place more frigid than the nights at this mountainside retreat had been.

"I took some close-up pictures of the yin-yang designs decorating the doorways into the stupa," Pei said, patting the tote bag where her camera was packed.

"And the awesome artwork inside?"

"Yeh-yeh. The multicolored ceiling design, and our mandala."

The mandala! Morrie would never forget the experience of laboring for hours with the other six retreat attendees to create a beautiful, many hued mandala using carefully-placed grains of dyed sand to delineate the artistic elements, only to dump the work into the rushing water of Life Creek, where it all promptly disappeared.

The teaching inherent in the mandala exercise was, as Morrie had learned, five-fold: First, to focus fully in the present and do one's best, because the here and now is all one can be certain of knowing, so when else could one ever do one's best? Second, the impermanence of all phenomena in the material world; Third, the folly of developing an attachment to impermanent objects; Fourth, the practice of patience necessary to place each grain of sand accurately is also necessary if one is to live a thoughtful, meaningful life; and Fifth, that harboring desire, in this instance the desire to keep the mandala, leads to disappointment.

Attachment also sets us up for the pain of disappointment, Morrie realized, knowing he was passionately attached to his sportcar, had been for ten years now, and could not imagine life without it.

"What activity did you like best?" he asked Pei.

"Circumambulating the stupa," she answered promptly. "Will bring us good luck!"

Side-by-side they had walked meditatively around the temple the prescribed number of times. When they began their third encircling, he had reached for Pei's hand. The child-like way her hand had clung to his surprised Morrie, and evoked a spontaneous, heartfelt, protector instinct, which further surprised him.

Pei's combined traits of insouciance and douceur fascinated Morrie so much that he looked forward to time spent with her, to either bask in her pleasant sweetness or be amused by her seemingly careless indifference. When she had expressed a desire to attend a weekend retreat at a Buddhist monastery where a celebrated lama would be lecturing and leading meditation, he unhesitatingly offered to provide transportation.

The highway intersection came into view. Morrie absent-mindedly hand-signaled his intended turn -- hardly necessary on this one-lane gravel road with no other traffic in sight, in any direction. He braked the MG to a full stop, accelerated for a curve right, shifted gear and inhaled deeply, relieved to be driving on smooth terrain again.

"Is it just my imagination, or do you sense a kind of brightness about Lama Trisong? Like he's some sort of human lantern. Is that what an aura is?"

When no response came, Morrie glanced sideways at Pei. Her head and right shoulder rested against the corner where the seat's back and the door met; she had fallen asleep.

Morrie smiled at the peaceful countenance that had, during livelier moments, lured him back to the Oriental Imports Emporium, Pei's place of employment, on otherwise unnecessary expeditions to purchase items he did not need. His stockpile of Chinese herbal remedies and teas would remain unopened long past their expiration date. But his attraction to this tall, large-boned, shy young lady with her blue-black Dutch bob, bronze-hued irises, full lips and dimpled cheeks could not be denied.

Neither could his studio apartment's lack of storage space. So, late one afternoon, just minutes before the shop's closing hour -- it was his tenth trip in three months -- he invited her to join him for dinner at the best restaurant in Chinatown.

When she did not immediately respond, but raised her eyebrows and stared at him with widened eyes, he feared, momentarily, that she might have felt offended; or, worse yet, misinterpreted his intent. Her rubied lips formed an 'O' before she voiced it:

"Oh...yeh-yeh." Abruptly, she placed an index finger against her lips as thoughts raced through her mind." I have to tell them."

She whirled and dashed out of the room. Morrie heard her rapid footsteps ascend the iron stairs, then soon descend again, the latter accompanied by a shrill, female voice shouting in a Chinese dialect.

Carrying a coat over one arm, Pei returned to the store, her face flushed; she giggled nervously. Morrie, who stood facing the curio cabinet, admiring his favorite among the Oriental relics displayed there -- an 18 inch tall, rare and beautiful, carved white marble Quan Yin, mythical goddess of mercy, her expression serene, eyes downcast, seated upon a proud and noble elephant -- wordlessly smiled and winked at Pei, stepped toward her and in gentlemanly fashion took her arm and led her across the room and out the main entrance.

His MG was parked at the curb directly in front of the Oriental Imports Emporium. They both pretended to not hear the loud argument issuing from the second floor of the market building. Morrie opened a car door for Pei and walked around the sportcar to enter on the driver's side. The vehicle glided into the flow of traffic...

"Can we make a stop soon?" Pei was awake.

"Sure. Are you hungry?" Morrie glanced at his wristwatch. "It's past noon, and we're still more than two hours from home."

"Yeh-yeh."

At the perimeter of the next city, Castlevale, Morrie veered the roadster onto the business route so they could find a place to stop for lunch.

"There's a China Table!" Pei gestured toward a side street; Morrie turned the steering wheel, followed her direction toward the restaurant, and the MG rolled smartly into a snug parking spot across the street from the diner.

❧

"You like cashmere sweaters, don't you?" Pei asked, helping herself to a second helping of hot red pepper-broccoli-garlic stir-fry to accompany the remaining portion of steamed white rice on her plate.

"I do. They are warm, but lightweight and comfortable. Cashmere doesn't irritate skin, like sheep wool does," Morrie replied, running a hand down one sleeve of the burnt orange V-neck pullover sweater he was wearing over a pumpkin and blue plaid flannel shirt.

"You wear them often, in many pretty colors," she remarked.

"I'm amazed that you would notice," Morrie said, washing down a mouthful of sesame-ginger-bean curd with a gulp of green tea.

Pei blushed and laughed softly before continuing the conversation.

"Maybe the yarn for your sweaters came from father's goats."

"What! Your father raises goats?" The filled fork in Morrie's hand paused in its transit from plate to mouth.

"Yeh-yeh, in Mongolia. Father, his father, and paternal ancestors as far back as we know raised Kashmir goats for their dense coats of long, fine hair."

"And he sells the hair to yarn-spinners?" Morrie was flabbergasted to make this unexpected and totally unconsidered connection with a favorite sartorial element, second in status only to the tweed -- blue, black, brown or grey -- driver's cap, without which identification he felt incompletely dressed.

"Yeh -- not directly. He sells to a yarn co-operative. They sell to factories that make sweaters, gloves, socks, coats, afghans, and whatever."

"Does your family own the land he herds on?"

"Grazing lands are public. The herdsmen decide among themselves where each herd grazes. In the days of communist rule, grandfather's herd was part of a mandated collective and the number of animals he could own was limited. Because he owned more than 200 goats, he was considered too rich, so many of his animals were seized and given to the poor -- then he was poor, too!"

Morrie smiled and nodded, expressing his interest in her story.

"Ancestors long ago were nomads, independent herders roaming the area, as were most of the population. Then, sons of Chinggis Khan established feudal system. For centuries, herdsmen had to pay a feudal lord some kind of remuneration for grazing stock on fiefdom land. They were subject to being called into the landlord's military service, too.

"Now, democratic government is reviving national economy by increasing private ownership; individual enterprise is encouraged in Mongolia. Future looks good for father; he may own as many animals as he can care for, and everybody loves cashmere!" Pei concluded and deftly maneuvered her chopsticks to transport the last bit of rice to her mouth.

"Is the wool sheared from dead animals?", Morrie inquired.

"No, no! Very poor quality wool from dead animal. Has to be pashmina, animal hair fibre, sheared from live Kashmir goat, from their soft undercoat, like down, to be so luxurious."

"How did the goats get from Kashmir to Mongolia?" Morrie wondered.

"You forget about the Silk Road. Ancient caravans met on the road and bartered goods, and the 13th century Mongol hordes plundered all of Asia for centuries. Even before that, inhabitants of the region were nomadic people, always on the move, taking animals with them and trading wherever they went."

"So today, most of the world's cashmere wool comes from Mongolia," Morrie commented, pushing his emptied plate aside.

"It is one of our major exports," Pei added, placing her chopsticks significantly across her plate.

"Do I have to actually eat the cookie for my fortune to come true?" Morrie joked, cracking a fortune cookie into halves. "'You are in good company' it says; well, tell me something I don't already know!" He smiled across the table at Pei, who blushed and giggled.

Perhaps in answer to Morrie's tongue-in-cheek question, Pei quietly and quickly consumed her fortune cookie before reading the prophecy from the bakery: "The nightmare has ended."

How could anyone know! Her brows puckered into severe frown; she stared at the slip of paper and re-read the message very slowly. "The...night...mare...has...ended," continuing to focus her eyes upon it, wishing to see different words.

"Well, good!" Morrie exclaimed, rising abruptly. He gently pulled Pei from her seat in the booth and held open her black pressed-wool coat, appreciating her height as he did so: She was almost as tall as his own 5-feet and 10-inches, and carried herself regally.

He followed her long, blue-jean-clad legs across the dining room until they suddenly stopped. She turned to greet a woman sitting in the next booth:

"Tanya! So nice to see you."

Pei's head turned to note Tanya's companion and address him, also:

"Ah, so, good evening!"

Both diners gazed curiously at the man with Sephardic facial features who stood next to Pei.

"Oh. This is my friend, Mr. Maccabbee. We are returning from --" Fearing they would conclude that she and he had spent the nights together if she revealed where they had been, Pei rerouted her statement: "-- a little drive. Morrie, may I present Miss Tanya Sokolov and Mr. Auden Lewellyn."

Polite smiles were exchanged, cordial comments murmured -- Lewellyn muttered something about their being in Castlevale to appraise an art collection -- until Pei executed an almost imperceptible curtsey and resumed her steps toward the restaurant exit. Morrie followed, but reached ahead of her to open the door.

"And they are?" he asked, as they strode across the street to the MG.

"Tanya Sokolov is retired fashion model, has big art collection inherited from Russian military officer father and mother who is descendant of distant cousin to Sun Yat Sen."

"I see." Morrie nodded.

"And Mr. Lewellyn owns Dancing Dragon Asian Art Gallery."

"That's the one up the street and across Pine from the Oriental Imports Emporium?"

"Yeh-yeh. Expensive." Pei settled into the MG's passenger seat; Morrie closed the car door and proceeded to the driver's side, looking back to wink at Pei as he walked.

Nice man, Pei thought. *Now there is even greater desire to stay here...should not have desire, just lead to disappointment...What did that fortune mean? How could a cookie, or a baker, ever know about --*

"Think that'll last us 'til we get home?" Morrie teased, turning key in ignition.

"Yeh-yeh. Thank you, Morrie, that was a very good meal."

Pei wanted to invite him to stay at Wu's and have supper with them later this evening. She knew, however, that Madame Wu would not only never hear of any such thing, but would no doubt still be in an angry snit over Pei's weekend escapade with a "strange man". *Strange to her, not to me.*

"Didn't Lama Trisong say something about doing a series of lectures on Buddhism at the Chinese Cultural Institute?"

Morrie asked, merging his roadster into Interstate highway traffic.

"Yeh-yeh. Is every Thursday, ongoing. He lives there, you know."

"At the Chinese Cultural Institute?"

"No, no!" Pei laughed. "In our city. He has a room above Tai Chi studio on Elm Street, next street over from Pine."

"I thought he lived at the Sangha Monastery."

"Only during the retreats and workshops there; some for public, like this past weekend, and some times for monks only. Is second home, I think, for Lama Trisong."

"If a stupa is a reliquary, a shrine for relics of the Buddha we were told on the introductory tour, does that mean that some of Buddha's cremated bones, his ashes, are actually there at Sangha Monastery?" Morrie wondered aloud.

"Maybe," Pei replied, after giving some thought to his question. "Does not matter, though. Buddha is there in spirit, by spiritual connection to the artists whose paintings, carvings and statues represent the Awakened One. And Buddha is there in the consciousness of all beings who are thinking about him, the Jewel In The Lotus. One way or another, Buddha is always there, so Sangha stupa is a sacred place."

They rode in silence and fatigue accumulated over their busy weekend retreat spent hiking forest trails and practicing traditional disciplines of archery and menage -- arts taught in earlier times when Tibetan monasteries functioned as sophisticated centers of education and creativity, such as the construction of prayer wheels: hand-held bamboo sticks topped with a wider, spinning cylinder containing coiled strips of paper bearing the words of chants or invocations which, like prayer flags that fly in the wind, are believed to carry the messages, the mantras, whirling to heaven. And, of course, periods of meditation interspersed throughout each day -- or, in Morrie's case, attempts at meditating.

It was late afternoon when they rolled into the Chinatown community; the metropolitan energy revived them.

"Is the Emporium closed on Mondays, now?" Morrie eased his sportcar to a stop directly in front of the store and frowned as he peered anxiously into the market's dark interior.

"No!" Pei exclaimed. She jerked herself upright in the passenger seat and bolted from the vehicle.

Morrie gathered her tote bag and overnight case from the floor of the car and followed her into the alley and up the iron staircase

Ben Wu, anxiously awaiting Pei's return, stood in the open doorway at the top of the stairs. *Uh oh,* Morrie thought, *I've never seen Ben appear to be happy but his face right now is a map of tragedy.*

"Pei..." Ben Wu began.

She brushed passed his thin, diminutive frame and rushed into the apartment.

"Where's Ma?"

"Ma gone," Ben whispered, and turned to follow Pei into the only home he'd known in his 62 years of this life.

"Gone?" Pei's eyes scanned the dim parlor and came to rest at the sight of an opened book lying on the lamp table. By any one of its pages, she would readily recognize the Tibetan Book of the Dead -- a text to be read after the passing of life from a loved one, to aid the passage of the deceased in its arduous journey through the underworld.

She faced Ben; mutual expressions of comprehension and sorrow exchanged between them. Pei collapsed onto the aged sofa, its wear and tear only partially concealed by a taupe silk shawl.

Ben moved stiffly to sit beside her, to answer questions she could not find voice to ask.

"Neck broken," he whispered. "Downstairs."

"She fell down the stairs?" Pei's fingers toyed with the fringe on the shawl.

"No. In shop. Not fall. Killed." Ben's voice remained soft and even-toned.

"Killed! By whom...why?"

"Maybe burglars, hold-up; police find out, they tell us."

Pei moaned loudly, threw herself against Ben and began crying. Ben held her, patting her back and moaning.

Morrie felt invisible and wished he was; because, as strongly as he wanted to ease Pei's pain, there was nothing he could do. Overwhelmed by helplessness, he unobtrusively set Pei's travel gear on the floor just inside the entry and descended the stairs.

His fingers closed around a small white box in a pocket of his parka. The box contained a silver chain bracelet from which dangled a sterling charm of Hotei, the chubby, laughing Buddha, a souvenir of their weekend. He'd intended to surprise her with it this evening. *But not now...this is not the appropriate time, after all.*

TUESDAY

After staying at the Wash 'N' Dry only long enough to see his laundry sloshing satisfactorily in a washing machine, Morrie proceeded to the veterinarian clinic where he had left Fair Rhett to spend the previous weekend in the loving care of the vet's staff, all of whom adored the beguiling ferret.

"Oh, no! You're going to take him away!" the doctor's assistant exclaimed, and turned to fetch Morrie's pet.

Morrie wrote a check to pay for the four days' room and board and handed it to the receptionist, who smiled at him.

"Don't forget, we'll be closed next week, on vacation," she informed him.

"I suppose it's a good idea to have everyone on vacation at the same time; get it over with all at once," Morrie commented, taking the rocking pet carrier from the vet's assistant. Fair Rhett was excited by the sound of his master's -- his friend's -- voice, absent too long.

"Works for us!" the receptionist called after him. "Bye for now."

Fair Rhett voiced little mews all the way to the MG. Morrie placed the carrier in its travel position on the passenger seat and drove back to the Wash 'N' Dry. Preferring not to leave the precious cargo alone, Morrie brought the caged animal into the laundromat with him. While he relocated his wash load to a dryer, the one other person in the laundromat this morning approached Fair Rhett's carrier and squatted to peer into it, asking:

"Okay to pet your beastie?"

"Um, no. He's kind of shy and might bite," Morrie fibbed.

A quick study of the fellow whose apparel had obviously seen better days, as had the unshaven man himself, led Morrie to conclude that there was possibly a greater likelihood of Fair Rhett being the recipient of an unwelcome bug than the usual animal to human infestation process.

"What's its name?" the impoverished, middle-aged man asked.

"Fair Rhett," Morrie answered, taking a seat next to the carrier.

"I know it's a ferret," the fellow said, looking up at Morrie; "but what's its name?"

"His name is Fair Rhett. F-A-I-R R-H-E-T-T" Morrie spelled the words.

Beneath his knitted ski cap, the man frowned briefly as he contemplated the pun, then grinned, revealing stained teeth and a vacancy where a lower front tooth should be.

"I see. That's pretty good. What's your name?"

"Morrie. What's yours?"

"Just call me Suds."

Suds! That's the misnomer of the century! Morrie thought. *This guy hasn't seen soap since Noah parked the ark.*

"So, do you, ah, live around here, Suds?"

"Yep. Right here." The man rose and seated himself next to Morrie, who suddenly decided he needed to be elsewhere.

"Time to take my perma-press shirts out of the dryer," he said, and went to do so, adding: "I don't think I've ever seen you in here before."

"Been here about a week now. Just nights, usually. So cold lately, I've been late gettin' started. Nobody ever comes here until nine o'clock or so, anyway."

Leaning against a washing machine, Morrie looked the man up and down. *Fifties, maybe...seems in fairly good health...been on the street a long time, if the condition of his rumpled corduroy pants and moth-eaten wool lumberjack-checked shirt jacket was any clue.*

"Started? Getting started with what?" Morrie pressed for an explanation of the homeless man's remark.

"Hustlin', panhandlin' -- you know. A man does what he can, takes one day at a time, minute-by-minute. The present moment is all anyone can know."

How Buddhist! Morrie mused; tossing his clean laundry from dryer to the plastic basket that had transported the items from his apartment earlier that morning.

"Maybe you'd do a little better if your clothes were cleaner," Morrie suggested, getting quarters from the dollar-changing machine. "Maybe in the middle of the night, when you can be sure no one will be coming in here, you might launder everything you're wearing." He emphasized the word 'everything.'

Morrie carried his filled laundry basket to his MG, placed it on the floor in front of the passenger seat, and quickly returned for Fair Rhett.

"You're probably right, Mister; but whatever I can collect is always barely enough for a few bites to eat, nothing more."

"I suppose so," Morrie said, handing a fistful of quarters to the indigent fellow. "This is for your laundry."

"All right!" The man's blood-shot, watering eyes beamed with gratitude. "Thank you, Mister. I'll do it!"

Back home, Morrie let Fair Rhett run loose through the compact studio apartment while he returned the newly laundered items to assigned storage spaces and warmed, for his lunch, the leftovers he'd brought home from the meal at

China Table yesterday. *I should have ordered a meat entree for F'Rhett,* he thought, then immediately realized *no, it would be too salty, too spicy, for him.* Thoughts of yesterday naturally included thoughts of Pei. He wanted to speak with her, to assure her that he had not abandoned their friendship; but he also did not want to intrude during her necessary adjustment to the tragic loss of her close friend and employer, Madame Wu.

He knew from their many conversations that she had been living with Ben and his wife for about two years now, since arriving from Beijing as one in a group of environmental activists from China. They were in this country to attend a month-long internship with U.S. environmental organizations. The project was part of an exchange program tailored to encourage a burgeoning public role in shaping China's environmental policies.

Attended by lawyers and activists, the curriculum had included a seminar on mediation and arbitration, in addition to legal advocacy training. When they returned to China, attendees had filed successful lawsuits on behalf of fishermen against paper mills and chemical factories that fouled the rivers. Others had been able to persuade the Chinese government to ban commercial logging in millions of acres of forest land.

Pei, however, did not return to Beijing with the group. Shortly after her arrival in this country, the asthma symptoms she had suffered in Beijing's polluted air ceased completely, and she knew a return into the toxic atmosphere would, sooner or later, be fatal -- as it already had been for many others.

Instead, she remained where breathing was easy, sharing the cramped living quarters of Ben and Ma Wu, who had volunteered to provide room and board for a member of the environmentalist group during the conference. They appreciated the assistance a strong, capable, educated younger person, with direct connection to the homeland, could give them.

Because she was on his mind, when his kitchen wall telephone rang, Morrie thought it was Pei calling.

"Hey, I miss your presence!" He said, into the receiver. "I've been wanting to call you and let you know I haven't abandoned you, but I didn't want to interfere with your mourning."

"Morning? It's one o'clock in the afternoon, already. I've missed your presence, too; you were gone the whole weekend!"

"Oh, hi, Mom. I was just about to return your calls," he fibbed.

"Where were you? I needed to tawk to you about something."

"I went to a Buddhist retreat," he replied.

"A nudist retreat! Why, Morrie, Dr. Stein used to write excuses for you to get out of gym classes in high school because you didn't like getting naked around the other boys for the showers!"

"Not nudist, Mom; Buddhist. Booo-dist."

Her reply seemed a long time coming.

"Better it should be nudist," she muttered. "You went all by yourself?"

"No, with my friend Pei," Morrie replied, pulling a dining chair closer and dropping onto it.

"Pay? What kind of name is that? It sounds Chinese."

"So what did you want to talk to me about?" he asked, preferring not to tell her, at least not at this moment, that his friend was actually Mongolian, and not a he.

"Oh, yes. One of the Rosens' cats is missing. Remember Tofu, the fluffy white one?"

Judge Lawrence Rosen, his wife Judy and their daughter, Michaela, lived in a house diagonally across the street from his mother's residence, wherein Morrie had been raised. The two families had been friends for as long as Morrie could remember.

"Uh, I'm not sure. How long has it been missing?"

"Friday, it'll be a whole week. I tried to cawl you. Judy would like to hire you to find Tofu."

I wonder whose idea that was, Morrie sarcastically thought, knowing full well whose idea it was. He was bored with hunting feline pets, although his recovery rate was remarkably high -- rather, they seemed to seek him!

"Well, I'm pretty busy right now, what with --

"Morrie! This is the Rosens' cat!"

" - but I'll see what I can do."

Arising to hang up the telephone receiver, Morrie discovered Fair Rhett, exhausted from play, asleep across his feet. He scooped-up the furry little mammal, carried him to his habitat and gently placed him in the pet hammock, only to see him awaken when the 'phone rang again.

"Maccabbee here." He was taking no chances, this time.

"It's Mike, Morrie. How're you doing?"

"Fine. But I'm not up for tennis this afternoon. I'm expecting a call." That was true; he was hoping Pei would call.

"No, I can't play today, either. This is about something else, a new case. You have a few minutes?"

Mike Lerner had been a tennis buddy of Morrie's since grade school days, and, more currently, his partner in doubles matches. A discreet social services counselor, Lerner seldom mentioned his caseload.

"Sure. What's up?" Morrie replied, again drawing a dining chair closer and seating himself.

"This kid was recently picked up for breaking into a house, apparently attempted burglary. He's been released from juvenile detention because he's the sole caregiver for an ailing grandfather."

"How old is he?" Morrie inquired.

"I don't know how old the grandfather is, but Kim, the boy, is sixteen."

"Okay, go on."

"He seems like a really nice kid. Well-mannered, soft-spoken, no previous record of delinquency. But he apparently got himself involved with a gang of boys who do have records."

"Uh-huh," Morrie acknowledged, wondering why he needed to know all this.

"Well, the thing is, the boy said he liked to dance, and when I mentioned that I know someone who folk danced, his eyes lit up like I'd given him the keys to a brand new pick-up truck. So, I was thinking maybe if he could get involved in something he liked to do, he'd quit doing things he really doesn't want to be doing."

"Direct him away from the gang and toward a wholesome social atmosphere," Morrie deduced.

"Exactly!" Mike explained, relieved that his good friend understood the gist of his communication.

"You'd like me to take him folk dancing with me," Morrie prompted.

"Exactly," Mike repeated.

"Sure. Always happy to spread the faith," Morrie assured him. "Do you have a 'phone number for -- what's his name, again?"

"It's Kim. I can't give you his number without his permission, but I'll be seeing him later this afternoon and I'll ask him if he wants to go. I didn't want to mention the possibility of a chance to join a folk dance group until I ran the idea past you. Still Friday nights, right?"

"Yes. Can you tell me, generally, where he lives?" Morrie was thinking *just how far out of my way will I have to drive to pick-up this twinkle-toed juvenile delinquent.*

"He lives in the Chinatown district."

WEDNESDAY

Gingerly, to avoid burning her fingertips in the sizzling peanut oil, Pei placed four strips of tempeh in a cast-iron skillet, broke two eggs into a small, spouted bowl and mixed in a few drops of water. Returning her attention to the browning slices of fermented soybean loaf, she removed a spatula from the rack above the stove and turned the hot strips. While the tempeh browned, she chopped a fresh, green onion into circles on a cutting board. Sensing the tempeh was on the verge of scorching, she pushed them to an edge of the pan with the spatula and poured the eggs into the space vacated by the tempeh strips. She lightly scrambled them and sprinkled the mini-discs of onion over the eggs.

How peaceful it is without Ms. Wu around, yelling, Pei thought, turning to place her skillet breakfast on a hot mat on the scarred wood dining table that stood parallel to the short kitchen counter. The pot of hot tea was already there. The counter of yellowing, wear-chipped ceramic tiles ended at one end with an outdated electric range; a loudly complaining refrigerator walled the opposite end. With but two feet of counter space on each side, a single-basin porcelain sink was

35

centered; one faucet arched above it, and experienced manipulation of the two separate control knobs flanking it was necessary to attain any desired water temperature.

Pei pulled one of the four straight-backed wood chairs away from the table and was about to sit on the hard, bare seat. *No more suffering!* she reminded herself, and stepped into the adjacent parlor where she picked up one of the embroidered toss pillows that rested on the sofa. Returning to the kitchen, she placed the cushion on the chair and seated herself upon it. *"Nobody sit on Ma's pretty handiwork!"* Pei's mind replayed Madame Wu's words, spoken in anger when Pei, many months ago, had attempted to eliminate the back pain caused by sitting on the hard-surfaced chair seats. Ma had pushed Pei from the chair, snatched the pillow with its precious - *precious only to her*, Pei was certain - hand-embroidered cover and returned it to its assigned position on the sofa.

When Pei had offered to purchase some chair cushions, Ma had objected, dictating: "Pillows not belong in kitchen. Get soup on them."

Tomorrow, will buy four chair cushions, Pei decided. *Flowered. No, maybe Ben would not like flowers. Plaid is nice, colorful. Will just have to see what is available.*

With industrious application of chopsticks, Pei consumed her breakfast. She poured a cup of tea and carried it, and the precious pillow, into the parlor, where she curled her legs beneath her on the sofa.

So peaceful now...Ben gone someplace with Fay Ming. She had heard Ben and Fay talking in the apartment earlier this morning, before she arose; perhaps their voices had awakened her. *Ben very happy for a man whose wife was just murdered,* Pei thought, although she was all too well aware of Ma's frequent barrage of complaints directed at him, too. *I am glad she is gone*, Pei admitted to herself, letting her consciousness slip into memory...

Early one morning, before the Oriental Imports Emporium opened for business, Pei was carefully pouring loose black tea leaves from a bulk sack that had contained them during shipment across the Pacific Ocean into dozens of smaller, plastic-lined cardboard boxes which would, a few at a time, be available to shoppers. It was a monotonous, boring task; the tedium allowed for some simultaneous daydreaming. No harm would have come from that, if Madame Wu had not approached, screaming, suddenly behind Pei.

"No, no, no! Not now for tea! Open veg'ables now! Need more cabbage out!"

Startled, Pei had dropped the box of tea she was holding; its contents spilled onto the floor. Turning to face Ma Wu, she accidentally stepped on the bulk bag, pressing more black flakes onto the floor.

"Aahgh!" Ma Wu raised a tight, threatening fist at Pei. "You so clumsy! Why keep you, I dunno!"

"She is big help." Ben, hearing the ruckus in the market below, had come downstairs to investigate. "You know, before, just two of us work long days, into nights."

Madame Wu redirected her clenched fist and fervent temper toward her husband, wailing, "Why you not down here working now?"

"Write checks today, pay bills. You think that not work?" Ben replied, dodging Ma's fist.

"Write checks at night, open cartons daytime!" Ma ordered.

"Need to go out in mail today," Ben insisted, stooping to grasp the tea sack and pull its drawstrings.

Pei swept the tea from the floor into a dustpan, almost wishing she was back at her desk job in Beijing. *At least, I can breathe easily here. Ma Wu probably won't kill me, but the polluted air in China most certainly would.*

Stomping out of the market, Madame Wu vented her anger by banging her fist on the checkout counter as she passed it. Ben and Pei did not dare look at each other, did not want to see their pain reflected in the other's eyes...

And that was just one day's nightmare, Pei knew; *so many bad times like that.* She uncoiled her legs and arose from the sofa. *I wonder if it's too soon to get rid of Ma's personal stuff.* At the kitchen sink now, she washed her cup and chopsticks, scraped and wiped clean the iron skillet before setting it back on the stove.

Yes, I am glad Ma Wu is dead, she repeated to herself, pausing to gaze out through the window above the sink. Her attention was drawn across the street and up a few doors to the Dancing Dragon Asian Art Gallery, where Auden Lewellyn had just exited his shop and was crossing the sidewalk toward his late-model, black, Chrysler sedan. The sight of him called to Pei's mind the scene two days prior, when she, with Morrie, had seen Lewellyn and Tanya Sokolov in a restaurant *more than one hundred miles from here...long way to go for lunch! Mr. Lewellyn said they were there to look at an art collection...can't believe anyone rich enough to have valuable art would want to live in a tacky little city like Castlevale...seems odd...more like hanky-panky!*

"Speaking of hanky-panky, where have Ben and Fay Ming gone?" She spoke aloud and turned to saunter into her bedroom, a mere alcove off the kitchen. *So peaceful... this is first day Pei have building all to self.... feel happy.. think to write another haiku.*

She had become acquainted with the ages-old poetic form during her Asian Literature curriculum, and again when she studied Japanese language. The brevity and cadence of the style, and the fact that the lines were not expected to rhyme, appealed to Pei. In the composing of haiku poetry, she could succinctly express her emotions; it was effective catharsis.

Her tiny quarters allowed space for only a twinsize bed, clothes rack and tall bureau. She pulled open the drawer where her lingerie was neatly arranged and fingered through silk and rayon until she grasped a small, spiral-bound notebook. She carried it to her bed, and sat thumbing penned pages until she found the last poem, and was immediately reminded of the incident that had prompted her to write it. That was just last Friday morning, very early, before the Emporium's opening hour. Morrie would be there soon, to pick her up for their trip to the Buddhist retreat...

"No! You no go away on weekend! Busy time!" Ma Wu had screeched, after Pei had told her of her imminent plan.

"Never have taken even one day off, for two years now," Pei had pointed out. "Need to do this, need a break, need some vacation."

"Aaghh! Thankless girl" Ma, face flushed with rage, raised a clenched fist and shook it near Pei's head.

Pei picked up her cup of tea and retreated quickly into her bedroom.

"Go off with strange man, bad thing happen, you be sorry!" Ma yelled after her. Though she weighed less than 100 pounds, when Madame Wu stamped across the parlor she made the floorboards vibrate. "I tell Ben, he stop you!" She slammed the front door behind her.

Pei knew he would not. Ben was a reasonable man and, although neither had ever deigned to give voice to their sentiments, Pei and Ben shared mutual sympathy. She also knew that she should have told Ma about her plans for this weekend sooner; but to do so would have subjected her -- and probably Ben -- to a longer siege of verbal threats and abuse. So, she had postponed telling her until the last moment, preferring to minimize the suffering, though there had been several days of anxiety, anticipating Ma Wu's predictable response.

Sitting on the edge of her bed, notebook in hand, Pei had let the flow of ink transfer otherwise inexpressible resentment out of her heart and onto paper, thereby dissipating the hurtfulness;

Old woman still scolds

Not knowing how soon death calls

To end this nightmare.

Now, re-reading her words only a few days after Madame Wu's murder, Pei realized how incriminating were the lines and her authorship of them. *What if police detectives want to search Ma's apartment? Need to be rid of this!* She tore the page from her notebook and ripped it into shreds. Remembering her fortune in the cookie served to her at Monday's lunch in China Table, she placed the pile of shredded haiku atop the bureau and dug through the contents of her handbag to find that slip of paper with its incredibly prophetic declaration: "The nightmare has ended."

Pei's fingers quartered the cookie's message, scooped the poem scraps and carried all into the bathroom, where she flushed them into nonexistence.

THURSDAY

Just as she said she would, Pei was standing at the top of the concrete steps that led up to the glass doors of the Chinese Cultural Institute. She was leaning against one of the huge, cement-cast, classic oriental stylized lions, with their abnormally bulging eyeballs and fierce, toothful grimaces that flanked the main entrance.

Morrie swung his vintage MG into a conveniently available parking spot in front of the Institute and, taking the steps two at a time, joined Pei. Together, they pressed through two sets of revolving doors before entering the large main hall that was as wide as the building.

"This used to be a library," Morrie told her, "until they outgrew the space about ten years ago. The city leases it to the Chinese Cultural Institute for one dollar per year."

Glancing to his right, Morrie saw two groupings of sofas and chairs, each surrounding an immense, low-standing, intricately carved teakwood table. An elderly man dozed in a chair. A young woman, her long ebony hair tied in a ponytail, sat on a sofa, copying information from books spread open on the table before her. A bookshelf remained against the far wall,

43

filled again with books. At this early afternoon hour, a library ambience prevailed.

Morrie and Pei proceeded across the main room toward a hallway that stretched directly before them, halving the rear two-thirds of the building. At left, the first door opened into the director's office; next were restrooms. Mid-hall, on the right, double-doors opened into a large conference room. The last doors, one on each side of the hall, led into storage areas. The hall ended at an emergency exit.

Before Morrie and Pei reached the hallway, a familiar sound greeted Morrie; his head jerked left, his eyes searched for the location of the unmistakable clatter of Mah Jongg tiles falling onto a bare tabletop. He saw four card tables with four chairs placed at each; only one table was occupied, by four Chinese individuals playing the game of Mah Jongg.

One of the female players, seeing Pei, called to her and motioned for her to come to her. Morrie eagerly followed his companion toward the game in progress. Pei's curtsey was barely perceptible.

"May I present my friend, Morrie Maccabbee," Pei said, then introduced the woman who had beckoned Pei: "Fay Ming is the director here at the Institute."

The game temporarily ceased while the players scrutinized the stranger accompanying Pei.

Though she was seated, Fay Ming's delicate, diminutive stature could readily be noted. Her glossy, black, long hair -- tinted at her temples to cover graying -- was secured in a smooth chignon at the nape of her neck. Filigreed gold earrings studded with emerald green gemstones dangled from her ears; a matching bracelet encircled the wrist that did not bear a wristwatch. She wore a one-piece, long-sleeved dress tailored from a black wool-blend fabric; except for its Mandarin collar, the garment was of Western style. At 55, she was still a pretty woman, especially so when she remembered to stop frowning.

"This is Tanya Sokolov," Fay announced, gracefully waving her braceleted arm in the direction of the lady seated on her right. With her other hand, she tossed an ivory game tile into the center of the table and identified it: "Two dot."

"Hello, again, Mr. Maccabbee!" Tanya flashed a broad, persimmon-painted smile at Morrie.

At their initial, brief meeting four days earlier, in Castlevale, Morrie had not noticed how very attractive Tanya was -- or, perhaps, how skilled she was in her application of make-up. Blue eye shadow accented her sky-colored irises, a feature obviously inherited from her Russian father, as was her slender nose. Prominent cheekbones bespoke her mother's Chinese ancestry, as did Tanya's wide, thick lips. Her raven hair was side-parted and fell unrestrained across her forehead and shoulders; the ends flipped out and upward. Her long, well-manicured fingernails were polished plum today.

Tanya's apparel gave notice of her affluence: a triple strand of iridescent white pearls adorned a new-looking heather blue cashmere sweater set that clung snugly to her ample bust. Behind her, the silk-lined jacket of her steel gray worsted-wool pantsuit rested over the chair's back. A fashion model's career is short, but Tanya had invested her top-dollar income wisely,

"My mother used to play Mah Jongg," Morrie commented, "Sometimes twice a week."

"Here?" Fay Ming was astonished.

"Oh, no; at home, in homes of friends."

Tanya drew a tile from the play wall, glanced briefly at it, and added it to the discard, identifying it: "Green dragon."

"Ah, yes; want that!" The woman on Tanya's right exclaimed, exposing a pair of similar tiles from her concealed hand and reaching for the discarded green dragon. The cherub-faced woman made her contribution to the discard accumulation, called it "Nine bamboo," and rose to extend a chubby hand to Morrie, saying: "I'm Lily Wang."

Morrie stepped to greet her with a handshake. "Pleased to meet you, Miss Wang."

Lily was undoubtedly younger than either of the other females at the game table. Her jet hair was cropped short, both sides combed back across her ears, and uneven bangs fringed her forehead. No cosmetics had been applied to her face; her stubby fingernails were unpolished. The white-on-black floral printed Hawaiian muumuu worn with a hope of concealing her obesity did not achieve that objective,

"Do you own a business, Mr. Maccabbee?" Lily inquired, smiling.

Before Morrie could reply, Tanya laughed loudly and exchanged expressions of amusement with Fay.

"Lily ask everybody that," Fay explained. "She looking for work."

"No, I don't own an actual business site," Morrie answered Lily's question. "I'm a private investigator."

Morrie pulled his wallet from a pocket of his khaki chino pants, extracted four of his business cards and handed a card to each of the Mah Jongg players. Pei reached for one also, so he extracted a fifth card for her. So doing, he realized they had never spoken of his occupation. Pei must think I don't have any job, he decided, because she's seen me at all hours of the day!

"Nobody hire fat lady," Fay declared, perusing Morrie's card:

Mordecai Maccabbee
Confidential Investigation
Domestic/Criminal

"You investigating Madame Wu's murder?" the thin, elderly gentleman sitting across the table from Tanya unabashedly asked. It was his turn to play; he drew the next available tile from the play wall.

Conversation ceased; all four players focused a collective gaze on Morrie, anxious for his reply.

"No. The police detectives are responsible for that," Morrie informed them. "I am not involved." *And don't want to be.*

"Have you met Shin Lam?" Fay gently waved a palm toward the frail old man who had mentioned Madame Wu's murder.

"Pleased to make your acquaintance," Morrie said, extending a hand to Shin Lam. Knowing that a Chinese surname usually -- but not always, in this country -- proceeds the given name, Morrie was uncertain whether to address him as Mr. Shin or Mr. Lam.

The octogenarian's waning strength was evidenced by the tremor of his handshake. His long, expressionless face was thoroughly and deeply trenched; he appeared to be tired, weariness his constant companion. Beneath narrow eyes, fleshy pockets overlapped his sallow, sinking cheeks. He wore a trapunto-quilted, padded waistcoat of traditional style, cut from undyed, natural cotton fabric, with long, raglan-set sleeves and a Mandarin collar; at one side, a vertical row of twisted-cord frog closures. His loose-fitting slacks were of the same material, though not quilted. The bald top of his head was covered by a black sateen skullcap, which reminded Morrie of a yarmulka. What hair that remained, from ear to ear, fringed the back of his neck with fine, white, collar brushing strands.

His mind was still sharp, and decades of avid participation had made him a keen player of the ancient game. Shin Lam impatiently tapped a Mah Jongg tile against the table.

"Forgive for interrupting your game -- oh!" Pei remembered that Fay had called her over to the table. "Did you want to tell something, Miss Ming?"

"Flower!" Shin Lam identified his unwanted tile and placed it in the center of the table, to join the other ornate rectangles.

"Yes," Fay replied. "You big, strong, more than some boys. Want to be lion in parade Saturday?"

"Yeh-yeh! Would be fun!" Pei's brightened mien revealed her delight.

"Okay. Be here by nine o'clock Saturday morning. You wear big lion costume," Fay told her, then proceeded to expose all of her ivory tiles, reach for Shim Lam's discard and triumphantly cry, "Mah Jongg!"

Morrie and Pei resumed their route toward the hall and followed it to the first door on their right. Entering the conference room, they saw that three long tables had been placed parallel to each other and to a lecturn at the opposite end of the room. Four chairs, all facing the lecturn, were placed the length of every table -- nearly all of them filled now, at lecture hour.

"You take the seat at the middle of the table up front," Morrie suggested, immediately ascertaining that there were not, for last-minute arrivals, two vacant seats next to each other; "and I'll take the one at the table behind you, the end seat."

"Yeh-yeh, " Pei whispered, moving forward to the first table.

Morrie was arranging his parka over the back of his chair when he sensed a sudden intensity of light, accompanied by the same feeling of unexpected warmth he had experienced at the Sangha retreat whenever Lama Jigme Trisong Rinpoche was near.

The lama, in fact -- quietly, in slippered feet and his saffron vestment cloaked in a deep, rich red cape -- had arrived and stood behind the lecturn, beaming his perpetual smile at another expectant audience. It wasn't merely upturned lips. His entire, glowing countenance smiled: wide-set brown eyes, the epicanthic folds of which bespoke conclusively of Asian heritage, sparkled playfully; laugh lines at the outer corners of his eyes and the calipers about his mouth deepened; even his ears, flat against his head, appeared to be quivering with good humor. There was a golden sheen to his ageless complexion. His entire body -- a slender frame of average height -- radiated the contentment and compassion of a genuine bodhisattva, a being whose many lifetimes of dedication to knowing truth and bringing the joy of enlightenment to other beings had purified him -- he was enlightenment personified.

Lama Trisong's round face, its Tibetan features softened through daily meditation, was a study in circles: Round eyes behind round lenses of wire-rimmed spectacles; a button nose with equally rounded nostrils; two symmetrical semicircles of eyebrows; plump mounds of cheeks; the curving furrows parenthesizing his mouth; and the gleaming sphere of his ever-shaven pate. Now, his lips, parted to speak, formed an '0', as well. *The circle, a symbol of eternity*, Morrie recalled. "Today, topic is 'From Emptiness to Mindfulness'," Lama Trisong announced. "Any questions from last week's talk?" Not one hand was raised.

"Good!" the lama enthusiastically continued. "You have learned that last week is gone, does not exist. All we have, all we can know, is here and now, this minute -- which is gone, already!"

A few chuckles rippled through the air; Morrie grinned. Pei turned her head to observe his reaction. He winked at her; she blushed, raised a hand to stifle a giggle and returned her attention to Lama Trisong's words:

"Emptiness at first might seem to be a negative attitude, but opposite is true. Everything is possible for someone for whom Emptiness is possible. Concept of Emptiness challenges the traditional doctrine of no-self, which denies that there is any permanent self. No-self theory says so-called self is made-up of a series of momentary phenomena, which give illusion of continuity -- like flowing water makes the current of a river, or flicker of burning gas make the flame of a candle. By rejecting the idea that the personality is made-up of real moments, knowledge of Emptiness redirects the conceptual framework of Buddhism by also denying the reality of any momentary phenomena. Instead, everything is empty."

Morrie removed his eyeglasses and wiped the lenses on the inside ribbing of the oatmeal-hued cashmere turtle-necked pullover sweater he was wearing, examined the lenses through squinted eyes, and replaced them across his proboscis.

"...so, nature of all things is their Emptiness; all things are empty of real identity. Being void of real identity, there can be no real difference between any two things, no duality. No difference between samsara, the cycle of rebirth, and nirvana, the goal of cessation of suffering, and, no duality between the Buddha and ourselves. This means nirvana is right here; if we can understand that is so. It also means we are already Buddhas, because the nature of ourselves, Emptiness, is no different from the Buddha nature."

Lama Trisong paused to cast an embracing smile and allow a moment for the comprehension of his words, and continued:

"Full understanding of Emptiness requires balance between two truths: One, all things are empty, nothing is real, and two, from perspective of ordinary life, it is possible, however, to take things seriously."

Befuddled, Morrie's mind allowed his attention to stray to the consideration of the emptiness currently experienced at the Rosen household, due to the unauthorized absence of their cat, Tofu, who -- similar to the young Buddha -- had, apparently, decided to extend his horizon. *I'll drive over to their neighborhood and take a look-see first thing tomorrow morning*, he vowed.

"...so you see, by Emptiness, I do not mean nihilism, or nothingness, but simply the absence of inherent, dependant origination. Once this is recognized, the mind is liberated from the hindrance of conditioned thought and can now see things and events more clearly, freed to be fully in the here and now with whatever the immediate environment might be; free, to practice Mindfulness, from the moment you awake each day.

"When eating, for instance, with each bite be appreciatively mindful not of self, but of the source of food, gratefully mindful of all the many beings who made it possible for you to be nourished by it. Be respectfully mindful of its beautiful design. Take an orange, for instance; see how artfully it is constructed. When you pick it up, be mindful of the feel of the texture of the rind, how it gives way beneath your thumb when you peel it. Smell the aromatic oils and savor the citrus taste in your mouth. Such refining of our senses will hone our perspective and consequently enlighten our comprehension, which makes us all the more nonjudgementally mindful, allowing us to live completely in the present. When we live deeply, mindfully, in the present moment -- not for the moment, but in the moment -- we discover all the wonders of life and our pain fades away because practice of Mindfulness is catalysis for our suffering."

Cat! Morrie was again reminded of his assignment, albeit coerced, to find the Rosens' missing feline pet. *I'd better call Mom to find out if Tofu has come home.* For the ensuing few minutes, Morrie engaged his thoughts in a mental scheduling of the chores he intended to accomplish on the morrow. *Call Mom...find Tofu...lunch with Pei...pick up fresh ground meat for F'Rhett...take Kim to folk dancing.* His attention drifted back to the here and now -- a point, exactly, of Lama Trisong's lecture,

"...and to cultivate this moral power to the highest extent may take many lifetimes. Not to worry, you can always begin again, and again, at any moment. When Buddha meditated upon the way of releasing mankind from the grip of misery, he realized this truth: When man attains his highest end by merging the individual in the universal, -- through practice of Mindfulness made possible by awareness of Emptiness -- he becomes free from the thralldom of pain."

Lama Trisong's voice paused momentarily. He pressed his palms together before his chest and delivered the brief benediction that concluded every lecture; most of the audience joined him in recitation:

"May I free my mind from greed, hatred and delusion, for the benefit of myself and for the sake of all beings."

"Buddha-mind," the lama reminded, tenderly tapping his fingertips against his heart and smiling broadly, his eyes aglow with radiant compassion; "Buddha-mind."

FRIDAY

Morrie swerved his roadster gently right and braked at the curb in front of the house directly behind the Rosen home. He stepped out of the MG, felt the chill of a grey, winter morning, and reached across the driver's seat to retrieve his parka. Zipping the jacket, he headed for the sidewalk. Crossing the parking strip, his loafers crunched a path across frosted grass.

He sauntered along the concrete, gazing intently at each residence in this block of upper-middle class homes. To anyone who might be watching, he appeared to be admiring the well-groomed landscaping that enhanced each property; or, perhaps studying the early 20th-century architecture of these two and three-story quality homes, constructed before material and labor became expensive, at a time when pride-of-workmanship still motivated builders.

At the second house from the corner, an array of newspapers caught Morrie's eye. *Looks like none has been touched since landing on the veranda*, he observed.

Curious, he followed the walkway leading to the porch, took the stairs two at a step and peeked into one of the windows that flanked the front door. *Vacant!* He stepped to

57

look into the window on the other side of the entrance. *Not a speck of furniture...they've moved out, but the paper delivery person didn't get word of that fact.* He stooped to examine the dates printed on each issue of The Daily Herald. There were seven of them, dated back consecutively a full week from today. *About the same number of days that Tofu has been missing...hmmm.*

Morrie left the veranda and began reconnaissance around the house. The cloudbank had opened to allow passage of some sun; not enough to be very warming, but enough to reduce frost to a glistening layer of dew on every leaf of the foundation shrubbery. Passing the slanting doors to the cellar, he instinctively paused.

"Meeyerl!"

Morrie inhaled deeply, smiled, exhaled and bent to slide the latch that sealed the cellar hatch.

"Meeyerl!"

"Okay, okay! I am hurrying!" Morrie laughed and pulled open one of the double doors.

"Myrl." Tofu reposed on the fourth step from the top, looking up, wide-eyed, at Morrie.

"You're welcome," Morrie responded, crouching to pick-up the cat, who stiffly yet eagerly climbed the remaining steps into the outstretched arms of his old friend and former neighbor.

With one hand, Morrie managed to reclose and latch the cellar hatch; the other hand held Tofu securely against his chest -- not that the truant feline showed any sign of wanting to be elsewhere.

"So you came over here last week to watch a big moving van load up with household stuff, and were accidentally incarcerated," Morrie deduced aloud as he retraced his route up the street.

Only Tofu knew for sure, and he wasn't telling, only purring.

Hoping to avoid being seen by either Judy or her husband, Judge Lawrence Rosen, Morrie opted to leave his vehicle where he had parked it and return the Rosens' pet via backyards, on foot. *If they see me, they will insist on paying me,* he knew. *No way am I going to consider that doing a favor for friends is an income opportunity.*

With his armful of a contented mass of white fur, Morrie approached the new decking across the rear of the Rosen family's home. Passing the swimming pool, covered for the winter, he felt Tofu stir; the cat was aware of familiar territory. Morrie tightened his grip, in case the animal had decided it wasn't ready to go home just yet, and tried to bolt.

On the deck now, on bent knee before the pet door that he knew led into a laundry room, Morrie pressed the semi-willing Tofu against the flexible flap and through the opening. *The metal door that slides to close the opening and keep Tofu in is on the other, inside, of course, where I can't get at it,* Morrie thought, looking around for something he could use to block any exit Tofu might attempt in the near future. Two five-gallon bottles of spring water had been delivered, placed against the house, earlier that morning. Bracing the pet door flap with one foot, Morrie leaned forward and dragged one of the bottles over to stand snugly in front of the pet door. *That should do it!*

Cutting across yards again, Morrie briskly strode back to his vintage sportcar.

✤

"Yeh-yeh, come on in!" Pei called from the kitchen of the Wu apartment to Morrie, who stood rapping on the front door; it was ajar, despite an outdoor temperature of 45°F. For Pei, accustomed to Mongolian winters, this was not a cold day.

"Am I too early?" Morrie asked, crossing a dimly lit parlor to stand beside Pei, who was attentively filling two small ceramic bowls with a clear, ginger-spiced chicken broth dotted with golden splotches of oil.

"If I am, maybe I can help with something," he added, draping his parka over the straight back of a dining chair. New seat pads sporting white polka dots on red background made the chairs almost comfortable and contributed a modicum of cheer among the anachronistic dowdy furnishings that served the Wu family.

"Set table, maybe," Pei replied, gesturing toward a cabinet where dishes were stored.

"Where's Ben?" Morrie inquired, wondering if he would have to wrestle with chopsticks.

"Gone with Fay Ming. Again." Pei said, pulling open a drawer containing flatware, including forks and spoons, as if she had read his mind.

"Doesn't look like he plans to re-open the Emporium any time soon," Morrie mused.

"No mention so," Pei remarked, scooping steaming rice from a pot on the aged stove into a porcelain serving bowl. "Vacation time just fine. Do other things, for a change."

"What have the police detectives found, so far?"

"They don't say," Pei replied, removing a platter of plump dumplings from the oven and placing it on the dining table.

"Is this a Mongolian recipe?" Morrie asked, inhaling the enticing aroma wafting from the platter.

"Yeh-yeh. Called buuz. Has chopped mutton, paprika, cumin and marjoram inside. Very popular in Mongolia."

Pei returned to the oven and withdrew a large, shallow bowl of carrot sticks and cabbage wedges that exuded aroma of the flavorful fatty lamb juices in which the vegetables had simmered.

Ubiquitously, a pot of tea already center-pieced the white percale tablecloth; its bamboo handle arching high over a stubby, broad shape formed by the wheel of an unknown Chinese potter.

Pei removed her apron and folded it over the oven door handle; Morrie seated her, then himself, at the table adjacent to the kitchen counter.

"Small apartment, no separate dining room," Pei apologized.

"Hey, I have the same situation, you know. This way, the food doesn't get cold making a trip all the way to a dining room!"

Pei stifled her giggle behind the palm of a hand that habitually rose to execute that particular mission.

They filled their plates with savory dumplings, vegetables and rice and enjoyed the meal in companionable silence for several minutes.

"Do you miss Mongolia?" Morrie asked, draining his bowl of soup.

"Mmm...no. Miss family, though."

Morrie knew it had been four years since Pei had left her family home to take a job as receptionist for an export company in Beijing, Mr. Lee, owner of Lee Exporting Company, was a long-time friend of her father, and well-aware that Pei had learned to speak Russian, French and mandatory

English as well as the everyday Chinese that was spoken in contemporary Mongolia. Mr. Lee was also aware of the fact that Pei had been unable to find a job in Ulaanbaatar, Outer Mongolia's capital city. Consequently, when his receptionist retired, Mr. Lee knew where to find a replacement.

"Does your family live in a yurt?" Morrie queried, guiding his fork in a round-up of the last rice grains on his plate.

"Ger," Pei provided the native word for the portable, wood-frame structure covered with layers of felt that provided shelter for generations of Mongolian families since their nomadic days.

"Grew up in ger. Ger still used by father and brothers during grazing months. Mother lives mainly in a big apartment complex in Ulaanbaatar," Pei told him. "It is a simple life, very frugal."

"It must have been cozy. The yurt, er, ger, I mean," Morrie commented. "What did you do in the winter when it was far too cold to be outdoors for any longer than you had to?"

"Read; Shakespeare, Tolstoy, Dumas, Tagore, Battulag, Lu Xun. No television out on the steppe, of course. And music -- no light needed to sing and play instruments!" Pei filled their tea bowls with red oolong from the teapot.

"Folk songs?" Above his spectacles, Morrie's raised eyebrows expressed his keen interest.

"What else? That's all we knew, and father knows many; some are very long ballads."

"He sang them so you and your brothers could learn them?"

"And played the morin khuur," Pei nodded. "That's a two-stringed fiddle with head shaped like horse's head. Bow and string made from horse's tail hair. Beautiful, mournful sound."

"What did you play?"

"Yoching, like a zither. Has two rows of fourteen metal strips on a board; strike with two hammers, one in each hand."

"And your brothers?"

"Sukkcebaatar plays shudrag, a three-stringed lute. Has very long neck and goat-skin covered sound box."

Pei took a sip from the tea bowl she held cupped in both hands before continuing:

"Dambadorj plays limbe, a bamboo flute with eight finger holes."

"Your brothers have interesting names. Are they, and you, named after ancestors?" Morrie inquired.

"No, not at all. Sukkebaatar named after war hero who formed Mongolian People's Revolutionary Party and led revolt against Chinese occupation in early 1920's, Dambadorj was a writer; father and mother liked to read his work. Pei was Chinese girl, mother's closest childhood friend; she fell from wild horse, died."

"She was trying to ride an unbroken horse?" Morrie was amazed.

Pei frowned and nodded. "Breaking horse is play, a game for older children. But this Pei will not have bad accident; have lucky star!"

"Right!" Morrie said, rising to gather Pei's emptied plate, bowls and chopsticks; he carried them, stacked with the tableware he had used, to the sink.

"Yeh-yeh. Mongolian belief that each person has very own star, lucky star. It begins to shine the moment one is born and disappears from sky when one dies. Brings good luck!" Pei explained, rising to join Morrie at the kitchen sink.

Side-by-side, both of nearly equal height; they hand-washed and dried the dishes.

Morrie braked his roadster, veered right, coasted in the parking lane -- after business hours, the curbside zone was free of vehicles -- and came to a stop directly in front of the Chinese Cultural Institute.

That must be Kim, Morrie correctly judged the youth sitting at the bottom of the steps. Mike had told him the boy didn't want to be picked up at his home, but would meet Morrie outside the Chinese Cultural Institute; and he had told Kim to watch for a dark green MG.

Kim had no idea what an MG might be, but when Morrie's arrived, Kim figured *that must be it,* and rose to meet the driver.

Morrie opened the car door on the driver's side and stood to greet the tall, long-legged lad who ambled, smiling, toward him. From a center self-part, Kim's ebony hair fell forward across both sides of his forehead, the thick strands ending at the outer corner of his eyes. At the back of his neck, his hair reached mid-neck. Between the draping forelocks, a high forehead was partially exposed. *Smart kid,* Morrie knowingly interpreted the significant facial feature. Kim's endearing smile curved around white, even teeth; his dark, almond-shaped eyes looked unselfconsciously into Morrie's eyes. *Good-looking, too,* Morrie determined; *he even has a dimple in his chin!*

Kim wore black jeans, white and black running shoes and a black, hooded jacket. Later, Morrie would note that, beneath the jacket, Kim wore a long-sleeved, black chamois flannel shirt, the collar open to reveal the curved neckline of a white T-shirt.

"Mr. Maccabbee?" The boy's voice was strong and self-confident.

"Yes, but just call me Morrie. Hop in!"

"Have you ever done any dancing before?" Morrie opened conversation.

"A little hip-hop awhile back. And I danced in my high school's production of West Side Story."

"And you liked it?"

"Yes. It's difficult for me to sit still when I hear good music." Kim did not confess that, in the privacy of home, he often improvised dances when he heard motivating rhythms.

"You'll hear lots of good music tonight," Morrie assured him. "Melodies from many cultures."

Music of the first dance, predictably an easy one, began just as Morrie and Kim entered the gymnasium. Morrie joined hands with the dancer at the end of a line and, with his free hand, reached for Kim's hand, telling him: "You can do this. Just watch my feet; little, bouncy, running steps. See?"

Kim eagerly followed and readily learned all the variation options of Savila Se Bela Losa, "the vine that winds around itself," the grapevine.

"This is a circle dance," Morrie informed Kim, next leading him into formation for an Israeli hora. "Watch the feet of the person next to you, not of anyone opposite you; that might confuse you."

By the end of the third dance, the Roumanian Alunelul, Kim was actually laughing -- mainly at his own stumbling through the rapid, demanding, alternating-foot stamping.

As break time neared, the footwork of more advanced, Bulgarian dances challenged Kim; he dropped out of the line and tried to follow the steps of accomplished dancers.

"Watch the footwork of people at the lead end of a line," Morrie had advised him. "That's where the dancers who really know the dance position themselves."

At the break, Morrie's eyes surveyed the gym, searching for Kim. He wanted to show his guest the refreshment table and introduce him to a few friends. When his gaze reached the table bearing snack offerings, he saw that Kim had not needed his help in that regard. Surrounded by half a dozen other teenagers, most of them female, Kim was stuffing cookies into his smiling mouth.

Halfway to the punchbowl, Morrie felt a hand on his shoulder.

"Morrie!"

"Hey, Vince!" Morrie exclaimed, after whirling to see who had hailed him.

"Are you busy next week?" Vince inquired, adapting to Morrie's stride.

"No, not particularly. What's up?" Morrie replied.

"Well, it's the annual Folk Arts Council meeting, in Denver this year." Vince ladled punch into two paper cups and handed one to Morrie.

"Uh-huh," Morrie acknowledged, gulping punch.

"Well, I can't go, after all. Baby due, you know. I can't leave Laura alone right now."

Immediately, Morrie perceived what Vince was leading to. Laura and Vince were long-time folk dancers; but Laura, obviously pregnant, had ceased dancing three months ago. Every year, Vince volunteered to represent the regional chapter at the Folk Arts Council convention. Morrie decided to spare Vince the discomfort of having to pose the question.

"You'd like me to attend this year?" It was more a statement than a question.

"Can you? It really is a lot of fun. Business meetings, sure; but the dance workshops are great. And there are lectures and exhibitions of so many other folk arts -- weaving, carving, decoupage, singing --"

"Okay. Do you have your airline ticket on you? And the hotel reservation? The club pays those expenses, doesn't it?"

"Yes, it always has," Vince said, fishing in a slacks pocket for his wallet.

"When's the flight?"

"Sunday evening. The return reservation is for early next Friday morning; I didn't want to miss our dancing here!" Vince replied, handing the necessary documents to Morrie, who filed them in his own wallet.

"Neither do I. I think Kim will want to be here next week, too. The kid is a natural born dancer." Morrie gestured toward Kim.

"Oh, yes. I noticed your young friend. Light on his feet, all right. Where did you meet him?"

Because answering truthfully would violate a confidence, Morrie simply took Vince by the arm and said, "I'll introduce you."

An hour and a half later, Morrie again swung the MG to hug the curb in front of the Chinese Cultural Institute. Idling the engine, he turned to face Kim.

"You know, I'd feel a lot better if I could drive you all the way to your home, instead of just dropping you here at such a late hour."

"This isn't late, not for me!" Kim laughed. He opened the passenger door, stepped out of the sportcar and onto the pavement, closing the door after him. He paused to wave a hand at Morrie.

"Thanks, Mr. -- ah, Morrie!"

"See you next week," Morrie called after the young man. He did not depress the accelerator until he saw Kim's figure vanish into the darkness of the night.

SATURDAY

"Om mani padme hum...om mani padme hum..." invoked the sonorous voices of the eight lamas from Drepung who had recorded the Tibetan sacred temple music emanating from Morrie's CD player. The CD was an impetuous purchase at Sangha's gift shop, while he awaited Pei's browsing; they'd made a last-minute detour from the path leading to the vehicle parking area as they departed the retreat five days ago.

Hail the jewel in the lotus; Morrie remembered the translation taught at one of the meditation sessions during the retreat the previous weekend. The throaty depth of the lama's oral vibrations surprised and fascinated him; he experimented to discover how deep from his own throat he could bring forth a hum.

Fair Rhett, en route to a hidey-hole with a toy in his mouth, abruptly dropped his cargo and stood staring at his human friend. The animal's pert cuteness was irresistible -- Morrie laughed and resumed his morning routine: breakfast of fresh ground meat mixed with kibbles and topped with a few drops of liquid nutritional supplement for the ferret, and the usual blenderized high-energy beverage with toasted English muffin for himself.

Thirty minutes later, the earthy, guttural tones had ceased chanting and Morrie was ready to leave his studio apartment. He scooped up Fair Rhett and snuggled the wiggly little mammal against his chest for a few moments before placing him into his enclosure, where Fair Rhett promptly scampered into his hammock for his first nap of the day.

Morrie checked to satisfy himself that the feeder bottle was firmly attached to the cage, securely resistant to the best effort of tiny paws that liked to keep busy, and that the water level was high.

Now, I am ready for a Chinese Lunar New Year parade! Morrie told himself, capping his black, curly head of hair with a blue, tweed driver's hat.

❦

Striding from his parked MG, he followed an excited crowd toward the parade route. Intermittent, rapid-fire explosions of fire crackers -- set-off to frighten away any evil spirits that might be lurking -- audibly guided him, as did the gong and drum beats, cymbal clashing and loudly shouted directions in Chinese from parade organizers.

Morning fog had lifted, but there was no doubt the winter day would remain very cold. *We're just lucky it isn't snowing*, Morrie thought, surveying the almost cloudless expanse of blue sky.

Limousines and convertibles carrying hand-waving political dignitaries had already passed by the time Morrie stationed himself street-side.

Resplendent in deep red capes and saffron yellow robes, a coterie of six lamas marched into view, led by local hierophant, Lama Jigme Trisong Rinpoche. Some sounding cymbal, gong, drum or horn, they passed, spectacular in the tall, coxcombic, yellow head-dress with peaks that arched forward high above the lamas' smiling faces.

The first artificial-flower-bedecked float rolled by, bearing the self-conscious and shivering teen-age beauty selected to represent Quan-yin, mythical celestial bodhisattva of mercy and compassion in female form.

Other mythological characters came dancing by, swirling yards of red, green, yellow and white fabric that constituted the costume appropriate for each: Yama, Lord of Death; Garuda, the mountain god; the Dark Old Man, identifiable by his black mask and white fangs; and other classic figures of ancient witchcraft and shamanism. Their immense, papier-mâché masks were studded with stones, metal, coral and much vivid paint in order to achieve fierce, exaggerated expressions.

Morrie easily imagined himself back in history, perhaps 600 years or so, dancing in a Buddhist monastery while wearing one of the over-sized, colorful masks designed to attract attention, be appreciated and make any lesson unforgettable. The lesson of good triumphing over evil was the usual theme of so-called mystery plays performed as part of monastery ritual in ancient times.

A life-sized elephant figure, representing Buddha, rolled past; hundreds of plastic white chrysanthemums (manufactured in China) covered the wire foundation completely from trunk snout to tail tip.

Sudden cheers from the crowd near him brought Morrie's attention to the next parade entry, a pair of upright, shaggy beasts with long, red and yellow synthetic fur: the Dancing Lions! Their gigantic, richly embellished, golden masks nodded at bystanders, encouraging them to applaud and participate in the performance by feeding them.

Synchronized with music of drum, gong and cymbal, the Lions' feline-like choreography is performed to bring good luck and ward off evil spirits. Bystanders show appreciation by offering "food" -- greenbacks, or dollar bills -- to the Dancing Lions in the act of choy ching, the eating of the green. Dancing a prescribed sequence, a Lion cautiously approaches the proffered green and before accepting it performs a few threatening steps intended to scare away any others who may want to take his green. With its mouth, the Lion takes the green and pretends to chew it. Inside the costume, the human hand manipulating the lion head grasps the greenback and places it, with utmost care, into a pocket; to drop it would bring bad luck.

The Lion head raises and the king of beasts dances happily forward, zigzagging the street, before accepting another bite of green. Variations of the basic beat keep the music constantly lively and the Lion footwork entertaining.

The other Lion danced on hind feet directly to Morrie, growling and waving its hairy arms and forefeet at him. *That must be Pei!* Morrie laughed. *Not to worry about her being cold in that cozy get-up.* Too soon, the Lions jigged on down the street.

Morrie made his way through the crowd and ran four blocks, following the red lanterns that had been hung from every light post along the parade route, to ensure good luck. When he was parallel to the Quan-yin float, he broke through the crowd to stand as close as possible to the paraders, to be prominent when the Lions danced by. This time, when one of the Lions approached him, he danced briefly around it before feeding it a dollar bill and heard Pei's un-lion-like giggle.

Again, he made his way back through the mass of parade watchers and dashed farther ahead of the procession. *Every few blocks, she'll see me...I'll keep popping out of the crowd to feed her!* And so he did, a lucky seven times.

The parade ended. Morrie sauntered to his roadster, his nostrils smarting from smoke and acrid fumes still permeating the chill atmosphere, residual of hundreds of exploded firecrackers. Cacophony of cymbals, gong and drumbeats echoed persistently in his ears.

He stood hesitating beside his vehicle. *What to do? Pei is busy with parade clean up. After that, she's going, with Ben Wu, for family dinner and Lunar New Year activities at the home of one of Ben's cousins.* Although he had not felt too uncomfortable in the 47ºF temperature, Morrie was suddenly aware of a warmth enveloping him. He turned and saw the ever-smiling, effervescent Lama Trisong approaching, still attired in full, formal, processional attire.

"You must be tired, after all that walking," Morrie said, returning the infectious smile. He wondered whether he should, or should not, extend a hand; his hand, however, did not pause to wonder.

"Ah, no. Long walk every day, early in morning, before anybody up." Lama Trisong shook Morrie's hand and continued to hold it, lightly patting it. "You are detective, yes?"

"Yes. Private investigator, not with the police department," Morrie confirmed. His hand freed, he dug in a pocket for his wallet, extracted one of his business cards and passed it to the lama.

"Ah, so. Thank you," Trisong said, glancing at the small grey rectangle. Gesturing up the street, he asked, "Have you visited Dancing Dragon?"

"The Asian arts gallery? No, I haven't," Morrie replied.

"Might find it very interesting...a very interesting, ah, business."

"Okay. I have a little time today. I'll go take a look at the Dancing Dragon right now!"

Lama Trisong nodded and resumed regal progress along the sidewalk.

Morrie decided to go the three blocks to the art gallery on foot. *I wonder what, exactly, he was hinting that I might find there?*

The Dancing Dragon Asian Art Gallery was empty of people; Chinatown's main attractions, this festival day, were elsewhere. Morrie stepped into the retail establishment, his footsteps muffled by dense, beige, wall-to-wall carpeting. He walked a figure-eight around the two pedestals that punctuated the middle of the sales room, studying the two vessels displayed at eye-level atop the pedestals as he circled each.

"Carved turquoise with Buddha and his chariot on the front, Chinese writing on the back. 1700's A.D. $900.00." Morrie silently read the description of one antiquity and turned to face the other vessel. *"Bronze dragon, its back supporting a pitcher. The surface has raised geometrics. 1300 A.D. $800.00."* he learned.

A collection of half a dozen intricately carved jade discs, most approximately nine inches in diameter, displayed on a ground of black velvet hanging against a wall caught Morrie's eye.

"Good afternoon, Mr. Maccabbee!" Auden Lewellyn appeared beside Morrie. "It is my pleasure to welcome you here."

"You remember me from our brief meeting at China Table in Castlevale last Monday." Morrie shook the hand the proprietor of Dancing Dragon extended to him.

"I was in Castlevale to evaluate a collection of -- well, an antiquities collection." Lewellyn gestured toward the jade discs that had been the focus of Morrie's attention. "Part of a recent acquisition. Exquisite detailing, eh?"

"Yes, but what is, or was, their purpose?" Morrie queried.

"Called 'bi', their precise function is not known for certain. These were, apparently, buried around 200 A.D. with a deceased person, a wealthy individual. Perhaps a status symbol, or some kind of aid to the soul on its perilous journey through the underworld, so that it might safely reach its heaven. Some 'bi' discs have been dated as far back as 10,000 years B.C.! A brief biography is inscribed on each."

"Sort of a letter of introduction into the afterworld," Morrie suggested.

"Yes; an object intended to aid the soul in some manner," Auden said.

As Lewellyn spoke, Morrie unobtrusively surveyed the exceptionally tall, portly man who wore dark brown dress slacks, a brown herringbone tweed sport coat with leather elbow patches. and a tan shirt, the latter widely open at the neck to reveal a patterned ascot of brown, aqua and emerald green. Wing-tipped brown oxfords, *probably a size 13E*, Morrie guessed, completed Lewellyn's uniform of the day.

Auden Lewellyn's narrow eyes, the outer corners slanting slightly upward, suggested an Oriental heritage. A tidy yet sparse goatee -- a mottled greying brown affair -- did not quite conceal a weak, double chin. The thinning hair on his head was smoothed straight back behind his large-lobed ears, where it curled outward across the back of his thick neck. His complexion was soft and pasty, his nose long and equinal. Morrie recalled that Pei had said the man was British.

"Are you an art collector?" Lewellyn asked.

"No. Just an art appreciator." Morrie kept a straight face, though envisioning the Playboy calendar; aging poster of the

Beatles, found, many years ago, when he and his mother had finally sorted through his deceased father's personal belongings. In the back of a bureau drawer they had found an unframed reproduction of a print of one of the several versions from Munch's "The Scream" series that, thumb tacked, filled the limited wall space in his studio apartment.

"It's never too late to start investing in fine art," Lewellyn advised, stepping to open a glass case containing an assortment of figures in jade, bronze and glass. "Some of these are priced at only two hundred dollars, despite their rarity." Lewellyn placed one of the figurines on top of the display case; his hands were large, pale and delicate, fingernails well-manicured to reveal wide moons.

Morrie, determined to alter the direction Lewellyn's monologue was going, correctly suspected there was but one other subject about which -- about whom -- Lewellyn would prefer to talk.

"So, have you always been interested in Asian art?" Morrie encouraged.

"I think so." The proprietor smiled for the first time since greeting Morrie. "My parents owned a fine art gallery in London. Even as a young child, I seemed to gravitate toward the Eastern pieces."

"Where do you get your inventory?" Morrie's hand swept a broad arc through the air.

"Collections, mostly. People need money, so they sell; collectors die and their heirs don't always appreciate the value, just want to be rid of items. And, I travel through the Orient or Asia every year, buying and selling specific art work my knowledgeable clients have requested."

"I recently read somewhere that there is a flourishing trade in looted antiquities, Has anyone ever tried to sell pieces to you that you know have been stolen?" Morrie's unpremeditated question astonished him; *why did I ask that?*

"Of course not!" Lewellyn snapped, returning the ancient figurines into the case and locking it closed.

SUNDAY

"Morrie, I have to tawk to you! Would it kill you to cawl me?" His mother's voice spoke from his telephone message-recording device. Morrie sighed, released the catch on Fair Rhett's habitat and stepped -- barefooted and still in pajamas -- into the kitchenette of his compact living quarters; the feisty ferret scampered after him.

Until he turned off the appliance, the loud whirring of his blender as it prepared Morrie's breakfast beverage prevented him from hearing the ringing of his 'phone.

"Maccabbee here," he stated, bracing the receiver between ear and shoulder so he could simultaneously pour the contents of the blender into a tall tumbler.

"Morrie, I need to tell you! Tofu came home all by himself!" his mother was elated.

Yeah, and pulled a filled five-gallon jug of spring water up against his pet door behind himself, Morrie silently commented.

"That right, Mom?" he said.

"Yes. That was Friday. I've been cawling you for two days, to let you know you can drawp the case."

"Okay, thanks." Morrie slipped English muffin halves into his toaster and pulled a jar of peanut butter from the refrigerator.

"Judy is so happy to have Tofu home again, safe and sound. She said he doesn't look like he'd been in any trouble, just hungry."

No doubt, Morrie thought, spreading peanut butter across the toasted muffin halves.

"Michaela said she saw you at the parade in Chinatown yesterday.

"Who?" Morrie bit into his breakfast.

"You know! The Rosen girl, Judy and Lawrence's daughter!"

"Oh."

"You didn't get involved in that Chinatown murder, did you?"

"No, Mom. I told you, the police detectives are investigating that.

"That's good, because the Chinese mafia is worse than the Italian mob; they torture you before giving you the cement shoes. Haven't you heard of the Chinese water torture?"

"Not to worry, I'm not looking for any killer. That water treatment was historical; I don't think they do that anymore." Morrie took another bite of fortified muffin.

"Well, then, you're not still involved with that Buddhist stuff, are you?"

"Mom, you know how Torah tells us to love our neighbor as our self?"

"Ye-es?"

"Well, Buddha said there is no self, so maybe we're off the hook!"

"Oh, Morrie! Morrie, you –"

"I have to feed Fair Rhett, Mom. He's looking up at me very expectantly." That was true.

"All right. We'll tawk again soon."

"Bye, Mom."

With his hungry pet brushing against his ankles, Morrie opened a can of high-protein cat food, scooped a portion onto a saucer and placed the meal in the habitat, leaving the cage door open so Fair Rhett could follow his meal and exit at will.

Breakfast dishes washed, futon made up, and dressed in Navy blue perma-press twill slacks, burgundy cashmere sweater-vest over a white dress shirt, and blue and white Argyll socks, Morrie began filling a duffel bag with items he would need during his four-plus days at the Folk Arts Conference. *Warmer there...I'll take the lightweight navy corduroy sport coat and leave my parka in my car... What happened to all the pairs of socks I just piled over here?*

Fair Rhett, clutching a pair of red and gray socks in his teeth, dashed beneath Morrie's desk.

"Uh-huh, I thought so!" Morrie retrieved his sock pairs from the ferret's hidey-hole and stashed them into his duffel.

"Okay, rascal, time for Jump!" Morrie, zipping the bag shut, told the animal.

His eyes meeting Fair Rhett's raccoon-like masked eyes, Morrie repeated, "Jump."

The ferret scampered to his toy bin and returned, dragging a plastic ring. Morrie stepped from the kitchenette with raisins concealed in one hand. He squatted to take the hoop and hold it two inches above the floor, a circle between himself and the ferret. From his side of the hoop, Morrie offered a raisin and commanded, "Jump!"

Fair Rhett leaped through the hoop and received his reward.

"Good! Good! Good!" Morrie petted the intelligent critter.

They played Jump at gradually increased heights until Morrie had sated his guilty conscience about leaving his pet again so soon. *But Pei loves him as much as I do,* Morrie consoled himself, *and sometimes it seems as though he likes her more than he does me.*

He returned his pet, who was ready for a nap in its hammock, to the habitat, secured the latch and checked the water level in the feeder bottle.

He slipped his feet into black loafers, gathered his parka, sport coat, keys and blue tweed driver's cap and picked up the packed duffel bag.

"I'm leaving now, F'Rhett. I want to get there while the egg foo is still young!"

Braking his vintage roadster to a stop in front of the Oriental Imports Emporium, Morrie noticed that a photograph of Madame Wu had been placed in the window between the pane and cafe curtain; pots of white chrysanthemums flanked the black and white portrait.

He had learned from Pei that Madame Wu's body had been cremated on Wednesday afternoon, with only Pei, Ben and a few members of the Wu family present for an abbreviated ceremony. *No white mourning band for Ben,* Morrie had observed. *I've never seen him so happy. Apparently, no one is concerned that Madame Wu might be negatively affected in the afterlife if traditional mourning customs were not strictly adhered to, or that her spirit might linger on earth and interfere with their lives. I guess they figure she can't be any meaner dead than when she was alive!*

Advancing two steps at a time, Morrie ascended the iron staircase leading to the Wu apartment, a bottle of rice wine in hand -- his contribution to the mid-day meal to which he was an invited guest.

At the top of the stairs, Ben Wu exited his flat, carrying a bulging plastic contractor bag. "Trash," Ben muttered.

"I'll take it," Morrie said, exchanging bottle of wine for sack of trash.

"Ah, chang!" Ben remarked, accepting the bottle.

"Is that good?" Morrie paused mid-staircase.

"Rice wine, chang, always good. Thank you." Ben vanished from sight into his apartment; Morrie carried the trash bag to a commercial size dumpster in the alley, near the foot of the stairs.

Morrie's second attempt to enter the Wu home was successful. Fay Ming, her diminutive frame tottering on three-inch high-heeled sandals with lime plastic straps, crossed the parlor, dragging another, similarly bulging plastic sack.

"Is this trash, too?" Morrie inquired.

"Yes. We clean out Ma Wu's stuff. Nothing worth keeping, everything too old-fashioned and worn-out to sell. Just junk!" Fay explained.

Wordlessly, Morrie took the sack from Fay Ming and made another trip down to the dumpster.

When he returned, the aroma of garlic, ginger root, cilantro and sizzling pork esters embraced him. He removed his driver's cap and placed it on the lamp table, noting that the Tibetan Book of the Dead was no longer there -- or any place else in sight. Ben took Morrie's parka and draped it across the back of an easy chair. "Welcome to my humble home, Mr. Maccabbee." Ben's smile was genuine.

"Oh, Morrie very humble, too, Ben. He still drives a very old car, not waste money on new one." Pei's comment came from the kitchen range, where she stood tossing cellophane noodles and snow peas with cubes of juicy, brown pork and mushroom slices in a large stainless-steel wok.

A chuckle escaped Morrie's lips before he realized Pei was entirely serious. The value of his historic vehicle, coveted by many, was lost on her; she saw the roadster as merely an old car, and appreciated Morrie's frugality.

"Pei say you are gummy-shoe," Ben said, motioning for Morrie to be seated on the sofa.

"Gumshoe!" Fay corrected; she was placing dishes, flatware and chopsticks on the dining table.

"Yes; but I'm not working on any case right now."

"That right?" Ben's brow furrowed; he seated himself on the upholstered wingback chair.

Even-featured and still handsome, Ben's deeply lined golden-tan complexion and habitual expression of worry suggested a man much older than his true age of 62 years. Today, khaki twill pants, a long-sleeved black and tan subdued plaid flannel shirt under a khaki, trapunto-quilted vest clothed his slight, wiry, five and a half feet tall frame. Oriental style black sateen slippers over black-socked feet completed his attire, as they did every day.

Fay tottered into the parlor. Black tights emphasized her thin legs; a long-sleeved, black, wool-blend jersey wrapped around her almost bustless torso and tied above her left hip.

"Dinner ready now," Fay announced, her crimsoned lips curving into a cordial smile. Behind her, Pei carried a large serving bowl containing the noodle entree to the table.

Morrie and Ben followed Fay into the kitchen, where the four took seats at the feast-laden groaning-board. The aromatic comestibles were passed: Savory stir-fried string beans with water chestnuts; salty pickled celery cabbage; dim sum presented in the stacked bamboo baskets in which they were steamed; a shallow bowl of sweet and sour sauce, another of plum sauce; slices of lotus root lacery marinated in a mixture of soy sauce, sesame seed oil, vinegar and sugar on an oval platter artfully garnished with scallion brushes, radish fans, tomato skin roses and carrot flowerettes.

"It is an honor to have you dine with us today, Mr. Maccabbee." Ben offered the bowl of noodles to Morrie, after he and Fay, as the elders present, had served themselves.

"The honor is mine, as well; thank you for inviting me," Morrie responded, deftly -- and, he hoped, inconspicuously --

shaking chunks of pork from a ladle filled with the main entree back into the serving bowl, allowing only noodles, peas and mushroom slices to reach his plate.

Fay opened the bottle of Shaohsing rice wine -- chang -- that Morrie had brought and poured the colorless liquid into four wine cups.

"Maybe Pei shouldn't drink alcohol today," Morrie suggested; he was duly apprehensive. "She's going to be driving my car later this afternoon."

"Chang high does not last," Ben insisted.

"By the time our meal is finished, effect will be gone," Fay agreed.

"I'll drink only one cup," Pei promised.

Morrie took a sip from his wine cup. *Kind of like sherry, maybe...omygod, it tastes like kerosene!* Alcohol fumes immediately ascended his sinus passage; before he could fully determine that the sensation was unpleasant, euphoria had taken over. He felt light-headed. He aimed his fork at a dim sum.

"Pei tells me you are a dancer," Fay addressed Morrie.

"Yes. International folk dancing, since college." He felt giddy. *Am I slurring my words? No more chang for me, he silently vowed.*

"We don't do many dances from China," Morrie said; "but I know China has a long history of dance. Artifacts depicting dancing figures have been dated as far back as 4000 B.C." He ingested some pickled celery cabbage, followed by noodles wound, for transportation, around the tines of his fork.

"Many Chinese dances imitate animals or birds," Fay stated. "You saw Dragon Dance and Lion Dance in the parade," Pei reminded. "Both very old."

"Mhmm," Morrie agreed, his mouth full.

"In military dances, soldiers, dancers carried weapons and moved forward and backward all together, one synchronized unit," Ben offered, becoming talkative and red-faced with his second cup of chang.

"Dragon is sacred creature, is most important; symbolizes power, courage, righteousness and dignity," Pei continued. "So, Dance of Dragon can drive away evil spirits, bring good luck."

"Perfect for the New Year," Morrie interjected, consuming the last morsel of food from his plate.

"Difficult for dancers, though. Need nine good dancers, maybe more, depending on length of dragon. All must coordinate their steps with each other, as well as with the music, to avoid tangling or falling," Pei explained.

"The same instruments that the Lion Dancers respond to?" Morrie asked.

"Yeh-yeh, same musicians," Pei affirmed. "A misstep by one dancer can cause ripple effect along the entire dragon, ruin what should be smoother, rhythmic movement of the dragon." She paused to capture the last bit of food from her plate with chopsticks.

"Timing between Pearl and tail critical, too," Pei added.

"Pearl is dragon's head," Ben contributed, nursing his wine cup.

"Pearl begins the dance pattern. There are many patterns to choose from, depending on what Pearl wants dragon to do. Not just accurate footwork, but coordinated hand movements, too. Each dancer must be able to leap, crouch, change direction or pace and recognize every cue," Pei concluded.

"All that must require a lot of practice," Morrie remarked, leaning back in his chair.

"And energy, too!" Fay exclaimed. Her face flushed from the wine, she drained her cup. "What about Mongolian dance, Pei?" She rose to remove the used plates and place them in the kitchen sink.

"Yeh-yeh. Dancing at festivals always," Pei replied, rising to serve a colorful dessert: A chilled mold of precooked glutinous rice mixed with red-bean paste, sugar, almond extract and cornstarch; the surface decorated with a design composed of Jujubes, dates and assorted candied fruits and almonds.

"Eight-Treasure Rice Pudding!" Pei proudly announced.

"Ah, so..." Ben murmured.

"Too beautiful to cut into," Morrie stated.

"But we will, anyway," Fay declared, pouring a hot, sweet syrup over the mound.

"You started to tell us about Mongolian dancing, Pei," Morrie reminded, digging into his dessert portion. "Do you know any?"

"Only one, the national dance of Mongolia, called Bielgee, or Dance of the Body, because in a ger, the yurt, there is not room to be very active. It helps to be slender!" Pei replied, between bites of pudding.

Later, when the dishes were washed by team effort and everyone had settled in the parlor, Fay urged Pei to demonstrate the Bielgee.

"Need music," Pei said. She went into her tiny bedroom and returned with an audiotape of Mongolian music and a portable player.

Suddenly self-conscious, aware that everyone present was watching her, Pei giggled nervously; her hand flew automatically up to cover her mouth -- the well ingrained gesture of modesty.

The music began; Pei stared into the distance, as if she could see all the way to her homeland. She envisioned the dense layers of wool felt that constituted the walls of her family's ger; the brightly colored storage cabinets, wardrobes and chests that stood around the interior perimeter of the single-room dwelling, creating alcoves between them for their narrow beds. Centermost, the metal stove that provided heat, cooked their meals and boiled water for tea and washing.

Pei stood motionless before her intimate audience. Slowly, her hands and then her head began to move. Extending from cap sleeves, Pei's smooth, bare arms gracefully swam through the air. Ever so subtly, her body began to undulate. Almost imperceptibly, waves of motion serpentined the length of her copper-toned silk, ankle length sheath dress -- both side seams open from knee to hem of the body-clinging garment, else the wearer's legs be severely constrained.

Like a snake, Morrie observed. *How does she do that?* He was mesmerized.

Morrie was nervous.

"Turn right at the next light, then -- " he directed.

"Yeh-yeh. Pei know the way. Drive Ben's van to make deliveries all over town," Pei assured him.

It wasn't just because he was always a little uncomfortable whenever he had to be a passenger. And he certainly could not find fault with Pei's driving; she handled the MG very well. It was simply because someone else was driving his beloved sportcar -- a situation he never allowed, as matter of principle.

But Pei would need more expeditious transportation than the public transit system to make the twice-daily trips to Morrie's apartment to feed and play with Fair Rhett. He had asked Pei to drive him to the airport so he could observe first-hand her driving skills and give her any last-minute instruction that might appear necessary.

"It's not too cold for you, is it?" Morrie inquired. "I know this car is drafty."

"No, no. Is clean air, good for lungs," Pei replied, easing the roadster to a stop at an intersection traffic signal and rendering a manual indication of her intent to turn left. "Beijing air bad for lung's, bad for heart."

"How so? I mean, it wasn't always polluted air, was it?"

" Always in springtime, when bitter winds from Siberia sweep across Gobi Desert, blow powdery grit into Beijing. Mustard-color haze lies over entire North China plain for weeks; sand so fine it sticks to skin and clogs throat if one doesn't cover mouth and nostrils with handkerchief or scarf. Good market for surgical masks!"

Pei expertly merged the MG into the flow of Interstate traffic. "Dust siege even seeps into buildings."

"Can't anything be done to reduce the sand assault?", Morrie asked.

"Some troops were assigned to plant grass a few years ago. Erosion much worse after government ordered removal of trees and brush in attempt to eliminate insects' breeding places. Insect invasion was not a problem until after government ordered killing of birds."

"An unfunny comedy of errors," Morrie commented. "No one actually lives on the Gobi Desert, I suppose."

"Oh, many do! Soil is very good, if it gets enough water," Pei informed. "Rocky, though, and windy."

"I've read that the Gobi is a veritable gold mine for archeologists," Morrie said.

"Yeh-yeh, is big sandbox full of ancient pottery shards, swatches of fabric woven in patterns more sophisticated than any produced anywhere today, papyrus scraps, bodies."

"Bodies?" Morrie was surprised.

"Preserved by burial in sand. Dunes mark tombs of Han Dynasty citizens who were sent to guard the edge of their world."

"Wow. I think I'd like to go there, someday," Morrie decided; "but not in spring."

Pei turned her head toward him and smiled.

"You said you had trouble breathing all the time in Beijing," Morrie prodded.

"Yeh-yeh. Pollution constant, for many years now. No emission control required of coal-burning factories or coal plants that produce electricity."

"Cutting down trees made that problem worse, too."

"Yeh-yeh. Sooner or later, everybody sick."

"If something isn't done to stop it, China's poisoned atmosphere will eventually spread and damage the entire planet!" Morrie declared. Pei merely nodded in affirmation.

"Know what was best at Sangha retreat?" Pei teased.

"What?" Morrie grinned at her.

"Walking in the forest; everything smell so fresh and clean, so pure. Very easy to breathe." Pei deftly wheeled Morrie's MG into a parking spot near the entrance to the airport lobby.

She values such a simple, natural thing as a walk in the woods, Morrie realized. *So do I.*

"Maybe could do that again," she hinted. "Maybe some forest not so far away."

"Yes. We can drive over to the foothills -- no, better yet, the Redwoods!"

"Can walk among trees?"

"Yes, and maybe through a tree; trees as old as, well, as old as the Mongolian steppes, probably."

"Air is clean and clear there?"

"I don't know of any place fresher and cleaner. We'll go there next Sunday," Morrie promised.

Pei's sparkling eyes and broad, dimple-creating smile expressed appreciation and anticipation; emotion was inherently difficult for her to convey by voice.

Morrie opened the passenger door, stepped out of his vehicle, exchanged parka for blazer, lifted his duffel bag and briskly walked around to the driver's side.

Watching him, Pei thought: *Nice man...happy to be with him...makes life rich again...Pei very lucky.*

"But right now, I have something to give to you." Morrie pulled from his blazer pocket a small, white box and handed it to her.

Hesitantly, she accepted it.

"Open it," Morrie urged.

"Ah...is Hotei!" Pei exclaimed, holding the silver chain, its solitary sterling charm dangling.

"Yes. Here." Morrie took the bracelet and fastened it around Pei's left wrist as it rested against the steering wheel. She looked at him, and giggled. Before her other hand could exercise the customary conditioned reflex to cover her mouth, Morrie bent forward and kissed the top of her pert nose. She didn't turn away, so he kissed her mouth. She didn't giggle.

MONDAY 2

"Wish Ben would open Emporium, so I can have dim sum for lunch again," Fay Ming muttered, tottering on three-inch high heels of her synthetic snakeskin pumps across the great room of the Chinese Cultural Institute toward the hallway. In her office, she placed the Styrofoam-boxed sushi take-out from the Japanese cafe across the street on her desk and seated herself on her desk chair. After consuming the first, hunger-staving bite, she pulled open the bottom drawer of the desk and extracted a newspaper. The local daily was dated one week prior to today's date and the front page displayed a crime-scene photograph of a Chinese, female corpse.

"The body of the wife of Ben Wu, owner of the Oriental Imports Emporium, was discovered in that establishment early Saturday morning by Mr. Wu. Full details are pending a county coroner report, but death appears to have been caused by strangulation."

Broken neck, that's what...old woman with osteoporosis, bones break real easy, Fay silently commented. She continued to re-read, for perhaps the tenth time, the crime journalist's account, all the while chewing sushi.

"Madame Wu may have been killed when she interrupted a burglary in progress. Police found no money in the cash register, although Mr. Wu insisted that he had filled the register drawer with three hundred dollars in small bills shortly after the store closed the previous evening. No evidence of a break-in has been discovered..."

"Humph." Fay refolded the newspaper and returned it to the desk drawer. She scraped the remnant of rice grain from the bottom of the take-out carton and swallowed it with a mouthful of cold tea, the dredge from a steep prepared three hours earlier, upon her initial arrival this day.

Fool woman! Get what she deserve! Fay's memory began to replay a scenario from the not-too-distant past. She remembered she had been sitting right here, just as she now sat at her desk. She had been studying pages of bids from contractors who had responded to the Institute's call for someone to repair -- replace, actually -- broken tiles in the restroom. Sensing a hostile presence, Fay had looked up to see Madame Wu crossing the threshold, her eyes and mouth contorted by unrestrained anger.

"Ah, Madame Wu, what brings you to visit?" Fay had asked. The sight of Madame Wu anywhere outside the Oriental Imports Emporium was always a rare occasion.

"Here to tell you to leave Ben alone!" Madame Wu had raised a clenched fist and pounded the air in front of Fay with it. "Ben my husband!"

"Yes, Madame Wu; I know that," Fay mumbled, wondering what imagined action had prompted the woman's tirade.

"You know that, then you leave him alone! He not available!"

"Of course. What is it that has you so upset? I have done nothing more than exchange a few polite words with Mr. Wu, when I see him in the Emporium," Fay protested.

"More than words. Talk with eyes. I see it, see you flirt with him, see him like it!" Madame Wu shouted.

Drawn by a raised voice, the few people in the Institute crowded together in the hall outside the open door to the director's office. Fay was thoroughly embarrassed and did not know how to end the humiliating confrontation,

Is it my fault if Ben is pleased to see me? Fay wanted to ask, but dared not, lest Madame Wu turn her rage upon her husband, who, Fay knew -- as did much of Chinatown's population -- already suffered undeserved torment from his impatient, cold-hearted wife. "Perhaps we can discuss this another time," Fay responded weakly.

"Nothing to discuss. You not come in market when Ben is there!" Madame Wu commanded, again shaking her bony fist.

And what if I do? Fay silently, arrogantly remarked. Madame Wu abruptly turned and marched her slippered feet out of the room, the awed crowd quickly parting to allow hasty exit for the ill-tempered woman. Seeing Fay reach for a tissue and dab at her eyes with it, the building janitor had kindly stepped forward and closed the door to Fay's office...

Contemplating Madame Wu's murder, Fay Ming recalled a Chinese proverb, *"If you are out for vengeance, dig two graves"*, and felt her spine chill; she shuddered.

From the great room, a clattering of game tiles startled Fay, She glanced at her wristwatch and noted it was *not yet time for Mah Jongg!* Curious to see who was so eager to begin the daily play, Fay arose, her palms brushing and straightening the front of her black, princess-style dress. Her wardrobe included two of these dresses; identical, they were her self-ordered uniform of the day during the workweek, though they emphasized her physical diminutiveness. Her mood dictated the accessories she selected: somber pearls, rich gold chains, black and white hound's-tooth-checked power jacket, or a stylish belt. Since Madame Wu's death, a cheerful, brightly colored scarf frequently draped her slim shoulders -- as it did today.

"Ah, Lily! Why you here so early?" Fay addressed Lily Wang, who stood surveying the community bulletin board.

"Looking for job. If there is one advertised here, there is time to go apply before game starts." Lily explained.

"Nobody hire fat lady!" Fay scoffed.

Ignoring the comment that she had heard many times, Lily removed a card from the corkboard.

"Here is easy job," Lily said. "Tai Chi place want somebody to answer 'phone and do mail-outs."

"Well, the Martial Arts Studio certainly does not want a fat person representing them!" Fay admonished.

"Pro'ly right," Lily muttered, re-tacking the card to the board.

"Fong's clothing store needs a sales clerk," Lily noted.

"You'd be on your feet all day, standing, walking, bumping into things," Fay declared. "You would not last one day!"

"Ah, Chen law office needs a secretary," Lily read. "Sit down all day."

"At a computer," Fay added. "You learned computer over the weekend?"

"Oh," Lily sighed, turning away from the board. "Maybe something next week."

Both women took seats at the card table and began to construct the requisite four walls of tiles.

"Maybe the others will be a little early today, too." Fay said.

Diverse in personality and education, the intimate group of Mah Jongg players had, nonetheless, over a period of many years of play, established an affectionate bond; the common denominator was their mutual addiction to the ancient game with which they shared heritage. Fay, Lily, Tanya and Lam could be expected to play 3 or 4 games every day; others would show up now and then, necessitating the unfolding of another card table and more chairs, and the scattering of a second set of tiles.

"Oh! Tanya won't be here today," Lily stated.

Surprised, Fay stared across the table at Lily, expecting an explanation as to why Tanya would not be giving normal priority to their Mah Jongg session this day.

"House cleaning, sorting out belongings, going home to Russia," Lily summarized.

"How do you know?" Fay was flabbergasted by the news. Tanya had given her no clue, no forewarning, that she was even considering a return to her homeland.

"She call me this morning," Lily replied. "She say time is right, she has to get away."

"Well, what does that mean?" Fay asked, not actually expecting Lily to know the answer.

"Dunno." Lily's broad, fleshy shoulders shrugged beneath her purple, polyester knit tent dress.

A main entrance door opened and an elderly gentleman hobbled toward the game table. His tall frame was bent slightly forward by the accumulation of disabilities of age; but these were mere physical afflictions -- his mind was as clear and keen as it had been in his youth.

"Shin Lam is here," Fay said. She picked up the dice cubes, lightly folded her fingers over them and gently rattled them.

TUESDAY 2

Pei was happy. Mongolian folk melodies emanated from her old audio tape player on the passenger seat of Morrie's MG. She sang along with the music.

This was her second trip across town this day to feed and spend quality time with Fair Rhett, something she looked forward to doing every day -- morning and afternoon -- this week until she would pick up Morrie at the airport early Friday morning.

Pei let herself into Morrie's studio apartment, kicked off her fur-trimmed ankle boots and hung her black wool jacket on the doorknob. She promptly unlatched the eager ferret's habitat, allowing him to run freely while she checked the water level and security of his feeder bottle and removed the empty bowl that had contained his morning meal. The bright-eyed critter raced excitedly around her sock-clad feet while she washed his food bowl. She picked him up, snuggled him firmly against her chest and carried him to the Papa-san chair. In black tights and coral surplice, she sat cross-legged, petting Fair Rhett and speaking affectionately to him until he leaped down and scampered to find the plastic hoop that he knew Pei and his housemate so very much enjoyed playing with.

They played Jump for a while; each time, Pei rewarded his performance with an earning of half a raisin.

"Let's try something new, F'Rhett," Pei said, returning to the kitchenette for another, different treat.

Returning to crouch beside him on the carpet, Pei held a flake of unsweetened breakfast cereal before Fair Rhett's nose and with her other hand gently rolled the reclining animal.

"Turn over," she told him, and fed him the flake.

Still lightly restraining him to a lying position, she moved another cereal flake in a circular motion near the ferret's head. His eyes followed the treat, his head turned, his body -- guided by Pei's hand -- readily rolled over.

"Turn over," Pei repeated, and rewarded him again. "Good F'Rhett!"

Again, Pei circled a treat before his eyes, gave his long, furry torso a nudge, and said "Turn over." He did just that.

After several minutes of training, Fair Rhett no longer needed a push; the cereal treat circling before him was sufficient incentive to obey the verbal "turn over" command.

"Good F'Rhett!" Pei scooped him from the floor and returned to curl-up in the Papa-san chair, nestling the tired but proud mammal on her lap.

While the ferret napped, Pei studied the apartment and the furnishings that identified her friend Morrie, who trusted her with his most precious possessions. *Trust is most important facet of a relationship,* she decided. She fantasized about what life in the apartment with Morrie might be. *So many books to read, new music to hear,* she thought, surveying the contents of Morrie's bookshelves. She visualized herself in the kitchenette, preparing breakfast, lunch and dinner for -- and with -- Morrie. She imagined how luxurious it would be to soak in the bathtub; the bathroom in Wu's flat provided only a shower facility.

Could watch television programs together, with F'Rhett, of course, three of us in Papa-san chair. Would be no dust, she vowed, noting a coating of film on Morrie's television set.

Is futon wide enough for two? she wondered. Her head fell back, her eyelids closed, she dozed...dreamed of walking through a dark forest dense with tall evergreen trees...the tantalizing scent of moist ferns and velvety moss enveloped her...the air was clean, fresh, and easily filled her lungs...she was trying to catch up with Morrie, who walked ahead of her, just out of reach...

Fair Rhett wiggled to Pei's chest and licked her chin, awakening her. She laughed, placed him on the floor on his back and guided him through his latest feat one more time.

"Turn over," she commanded, and rewarded him with the object of his focus, the last cereal flake in her hand. "Good F'Rhett!"

At Morrie's kitchen counter, Pei chopped fresh, raw chicken heart, mixed it into a portion of moist, canned kitten food and placed the serving inside the Mustela putorius furo's habitat, for him to discover later. Lovingly, she scooted the pet into his enclosure and secured the snap bolts on the cage door.

His pert, raccoon-masked face pressed against the wires, Fair Rhett watched her pull her boots on and slip her arms into the sleeves of her jacket, loosely knotting the ties around her waist. "Bye, F'Rhett. See you tomorrow!"

Pei was especially mindful and alert behind the steering wheel of a motor vehicle. Morrie had not asked if she had a driver license; knowing she regularly made deliveries from the Emporium in Ben's van, he assumed she did.

Midway between Morrie's neighborhood and Chinatown, in a residential area, Pei heard the shrill of a rapidly advancing siren. Her heart skipped a beat, then the rhythm of her heartbeat quickened. She glanced at the roadster's speedometer. *Going seven miles below speed limit,* she observed. *Must be somebody else...just pull over and let police car pass.* She braked to a stop next to the curb, idling the engine until the patrol vehicle passed and she could resume her route.

But it didn't pass. Instead, the official car also edged to the curb and slowed to a stop a few yards behind Morrie's convertible.

In the sportcar's rear-view mirror, Pei watched, wide-eyed, as the uniformed officer stepped from his conspicuously marked sedan, slammed shut the car door and strode, citation pad in hand, toward Morrie's MG. Pei's pounding heart felt unbearably heavy in her chest. She wanted to cry; but ancestral pride, ingrained through countless generations, could not permit that shameful release.

"Turn off your engine, please," the officer ordered.

WEDNESDAY 2

"Shut the door behind you, Bao," Auden Lewellyn commanded. "If anyone should enter the gallery, we don't want them to overhear our conversation."

Bao, a strong, husky Chinese lad of seventeen years, with uneven shocks of coal black hair in seemingly ongoing dispute about which direction it should grow, wordlessly complied.

From his comfortable seat in an executive chair, Lewellyn gazed across his desk at Bao, who, with unlit cigarette dangling from his thick lips, stood fidgeting with his cigarette lighter. Lewellyn frowned; a fastidious gentleman, he abhorred smoke and anything that created it. Of course, smoking was not allowed in the Dancing Dragon Asian Art Gallery.

Lewellyn's gaze moved to give the other boy, Lung, a once-over. Sullenly, his eighteen-year-old slender frame slumped in a straight-backed chair; he resented being called to a meeting so early in the morning. But then, Lung resented almost everything.

"Your clothes look as if you had slept in them," Lewellyn observed.

"Maybe so," Lung mumbled.

115

"Where's the other fellow?" Lewellyn asked.

"His grandfather's sick," Bao replied. "Can't be left alone, he said."

Lewellyn sighed audibly. "Well, I guess we don't need him for this job. We've got a driver," he nodded in Lung's direction, "and one other should be sufficient to carry. I think a window entry is the best approach, anyway. We won't need your buddy's nimble fingers to pick a lock this time."

Lewellyn pulled a sheet of graph paper from the desk's top drawer and spread it open upon his desk. Both boys leaned forward to study the markings on the page.

"Here's a diagram of the floor plan," Lewellyn said. "The library where the antiquities are is right here." His long, pale index finger rested on a penciled square.

"Okay. What are we looking for?" Bao asked.

Lewellyn opened the desk drawer again and withdrew three, glossy 5" x 7" photographs; each bore the image of an ornately carved column with squared corners.

"How big are these things?" Lung imagined the columns must be huge and heavy, undoubtedly used in construction to hold a ceiling in place.

"Not quite two feet high and less than five inches a side," Lewellyn told him, much to the slight-built Lung's relief.

"Light green jade, highly polished," Lewellyn continued. He handed a photo to each boy, so they could study and memorize the image.

"Over on Cumberland Hill?" Boa inquired, referring to the city's area of ostentatious homes.

"Oh, no! It's in Castlevale," Lewellyn informed them.

"Castlevale!" The teenagers unisoned, exchanging expressions of distaste. Bao groaned and began to thumb the switch on his cigarette lighter in rapid on-off repetition.

Auden Lewellyn frowned at Bao, took the photographs from the boys and, along with the floor plan of the target home, returned the pages to the desk drawer.

"Well, that's not much farther than the big city, where most of your jobs have been," Lewellyn pointed out.

Bao sighed. "Tonight, huh?"

"Yes, please. I have been in communication with the homeowners. They mentioned they would be gone from their house overnight -- but only tonight."

"Okay," Lung arose. "What's the address?"

Lewellyn scribbled the Castlevale street and house number on a piece of scratch paper, tore it from the pad and gave it to Lung.

"Leave about eleven o'clock?" Bao addressed Lung.

"Yeah. I'll pick you up, like always," Lung replied.

"You should be back here by four in the morning," Lewellyn stated, following them out of his office and through the Dancing Dragon showroom to the front door.

"Yeah; quick in, grab, and out again," Bao predicted.

"See you downstairs about four, then," Lewellyn smiled and patted the boys' shoulders as the disgruntled youths stepped out into a slowly dissipating, chilly, winter-morning mist.

Auden Lewellyn turned the "closed" sign in his gallery window to read "open" and confidently returned to his office to do some arithmetic.

This'll be one of my most lucrative shipments yet, he realized. *So very, very fortunate to have found those three rare jade columns from a tomb adytum...date back to 3,000 B. C. ...been on the want list of my China contact for years...to think they'd turn up in my territory and so close to home! Some obscenely wealthy industrialist in China who appreciates art, or perhaps, simply wants the artifacts returned home to their country of origin. Whatever, acquiring for him the objects of his desire is making me a rich man, too.*

Sitting at his desk in his private office at the rear of the Dancing Dragon Asian Arts Gallery, the proprietor of the business made plans: Close the gallery next week and take Tanya on a vacation. *Maui, I think.* He rifled through the

Rolodex on his desk, punched numbers on his telephone and conversed with a travel agent.

"All right, that's done!" He announced to no one. "The shipment goes out early Monday morning and we depart for Hawaii in the afternoon!"

Briskly, he rubbed his pink palms together. Glancing at his wristwatch, he noted that it was less than two hours until Tanya would arrive for their lunch date. *What's-her-name will be here at noon to mind the gallery, I can take the afternoon off. I want to show Tanya the pair of Song Dynasty silk scroll paintings I recently acquired to hang in my bedroom...she might even want to buy them...business and pleasure mix very well!*

THURSDAY 2

Lama Jigme Trisong Rinpoche awoke at three minutes before four o'clock A.M., precisely as he did every morning since the beginning of his monastic life, at age ten, thirty-eight years ago. After a brief meditation, it was his habit to brew tea and enjoy his first meal of the day, consisting of whatever was left from the previous day's meal. Because a lama is, by tradition, restricted from consuming food after the noon hour, he awakened hungry and retired early, relative to the schedule of almost everyone else.

His quarters -- a charitable offering, a lay person's act of renunciation mirroring the complete renunciation that will eventually lead to nirvana -- above the martial arts studio were exiguous, but sufficient for this lama's belongings: a floor mat for sleeping and a teakwood chest containing clothing changes. Upon the chest reposed an electric teapot; a brick of pressed tea leaves; a small bowl for tea and a larger one for rice and morsels; chopsticks; and a brass Buddha icon, the parting gift from his younger sister who still lived in Tibet.

It was one of two upper rooms; the Tai Chi instructor and kind proprietor of the building slept in the other space. They shared a compact bathroom.

Lama Trisong stood sipping tea and gazing out through the room's sole window. Hours before dawn, there was little to be seen in the darkness of night: Only silhouettes of trees, neighboring edifices and a few parked vehicles -- except for the area illuminated, however dimly, by a street lamp. As though in attendance at a theatrical production, Lama Trisong watched the unexpected mini-drama that played-out on the alley-stage beneath his window.

Peculiar...there is Mr. Lewellyn, opening the door to cellar beneath Dancing Dragon Gallery...two fellows getting out of pick-up...seen truck there before, but never at this early hour...they take some things, long bundles, from truck cab...Auden Lewellyn holds basement door open, young men go in, come out empty-handed...Lewellyn giving fellows -- money? Dollar bills? They get back in truck, drive away...Lewellyn get in his big car, drive away.

Lama Trisong swallowed the last drop in his tea bowl and prostrated himself briefly before a large reproduction of a colorful painting of Siddhartha Gautama that hung on a wall. Sitting cross-legged on his mat, he began his first lengthy meditation period of the day. When his meditating ceased, there would be sufficient time to prepare, make some notes for this afternoon's lecture at the Chinese Cultural Institute. *Maybe talk about silent wisdom, peaceful stillness of silent mind.*

After that, Chinatown would be awake, the restaurants open for business. He would take his daily constitutional, his ritual begging round, providing laypersons an opportunity to reaffirm the fundamental virtue of generosity.

But thoughts of the nocturnal activity he had just witnessed were not easily dismissed. *Odd...what was that all about, that it could not wait until daylight?*

The two occupants of an unmarked government vehicle parked, unnoticed, on the street a few yards from the entrance to the alley next to Dancing Dragon Asian Art Gallery were confident that they knew the answer to Lama Trisong's unheard question.

Shin Lam slept but intermittently through the night, the woe that weighted his heart reawakening him several times; it was not yet daybreak when he arose from his bed. He, too, began his day by drinking a cup of hot tea. Instead of meditating, however, Shin's habit was to walk for forty minutes or so before taking breakfast, to stimulate a lethargic appetite and keep his reluctant bowels moving regularly.

He could have -- and usually did -- exit by way of the kitchen door that opened to a small back porch, where a new washing machine and clothes dryer had been recently installed, further minimizing the porch's floor area. His grandson had purchased the appliances and paid for their installation with earnings from his job at a local fast-food drive-through burger franchise; since the boy had come to live with him, washdays were more frequent.

Shin's little wood-frame, board and batten house -- one of the original private residences in Chinatown -- was long and narrow, stretching from a full-width parlor facing the street to a bedroom at the rear. Sandwiched between were a small kitchen, smaller bathroom and now-crowded porch.

This morning, Shin wanted to assure himself that the boy was, in fact, at home. He tiptoed across the parlor past the couch where his grandson lay sleeping. *So innocent he looks...whole life ahead of him...maybe he turn out okay...maybe everything be okay.*

Noiselessly, Shin opened the front door and gently closed it behind himself. His knobby fingers fumbled to button his winter wrap: a Navy pea coat bought decades ago from a drunken sailor who, that particular evening, preferred to find his warmth in liquid form and needed the wherewithal to do so.

He was getting a late start this morning, but it was yet early enough that he had the sidewalk to himself; that was important to him. *No respect for elders anymore...'specially one who walks slow...walk slow, better to see everything...young people in big rush, no see things.*

Out of the residential district now, Shin shuffled past the Chinese Cultural Institute and observed with amusement the hoary coats of frost on the lion statues. He passed the yet-closed shops, some with softly lit interiors, others dark and cave-like. Entering the plaza park, he paused to appreciate the still beauty surrounding him. Koi swam listlessly beneath a roof of ice. *Do they know the difference, when there is ice and when there is no ice?* He admired the symmetrical branching of a pair of identically pruned redbud trees; the leafless weep of an ornamental cherry tree; the niveous glitter glazing the bridge that arched above the pond.

"Slippery," he commented, startling a flock of over-wintering finches from the boughs of an aged cedar.

Made brilliant by the rising sun's radiance, multiple branches of a red-twig dogwood shrub caught Shin's appreciative attention; "Lucky red," he mumbled, continuing his hobble through the park to Glister Street.

Two blocks later, when he paused for the pedestrian signal at Pine Street, Shin realized he was standing adjacent to the Oriental Imports Emporium. He had deliberately avoided returning to this corner for nearly two weeks. Hesitating, deciding, "Aah," then, turning the corner instead of crossing

Pine Street, he walked by the Emporium, its interior dark. He passed the shop entrance and recalled the experience that daily haunted his conscience. *Was right here, only much earlier, still night...restless leg could not sleep, needed to walk.* Reenacting his spontaneous movements of the last time he found himself outside the Emporium -- which, as it turned out, was the same night that Madam Wu was murdered -- Shin's brow puckered and he abruptly pivoted to face the opposite direction. *Heard door open...somebody rush out...*he pressed his memory to recall the traumatic event; *could be I saw...but maybe not, maybe somebody else. I can never speak of this to anyone, never...because maybe person I saw was truly who I am afraid it was.*

Tanya sat at the dining table in her condominium, a porcelain pot of freshly brewed Russian chai within arm's reach. She wore a black and yellow tiger-skin printed sateen kimono. Her legs crossed at the knees and one imitation tiger-pelt mule-slippered foot idly, restlessly, swung to and fro, more or less keeping time with the Rachmaninoff concerto emanating at low volume from a compact disc player in the living room.

Auden Lewellyn has seen the last of me! she promised herself. *It was good to be able to buy the art I wanted at discounted prices by letting him purchase the acquisitions for me, but I am through collecting. I have all the pieces I ever wanted...and I'm getting bored with most of them...perhaps not as bored as I am with dull Auden, however...I no longer need to tolerate that tiresome relationship with him.*

The constant movement of her foot caused both sides of her kimono to fall away, baring her legs -- unfelt because Tanya maintained an ambient temperature in all six rooms of her second floor condominium at a warm and comfortable 78°F.

More urgent, it is imperative that I get away from here immediately...should have planned this better... Nearly two weeks now...surely the police detectives must be getting close to the truth... And what about that Maccabbee guy who's been hanging around lately? He says he's not working on the Wu case, but, of course, if he were, he would deny it... Yes, I have to get going while the going is good!... Before the trail leads to me.

Attempting to assuage hunger pangs that gnawed at her stomach, Tanya gulped a third cup of tea. Her eating habits were a pendulum swing from food binges to starvation diets; her weight -- never noticeably excessive relative to her medium height -- fluctuated minimally.

She arose from the dining chair, scuffed to the guest bedroom and pulled luggage from a closet. The apparel and incidentals she had chosen to take with her were spread across the counterpane. She paused to cast an appreciative glance at the mask of Ka-Nefer displayed against a wall; Lewellyn had acquired it for her through a clandestine network of operatives: It had been stolen from a storeroom in the Cairo Museum.

Tomorrow, I fly to Tokyo...from there, on to Moscow...I can stay with my brother and his wife in St. Petersburg for a few days, at least, until I decide my next move...maybe London. She brushed stray hair back from her face and readjusted the wide, gold barrette to keep strands from falling forward across her eyes, hindering her vision.

Tanya meticulously folded each garment for its journey and began efficiently arranging all in suitcases. *I will be gone from this home for a long time.*

FRIDAY 2

At eight o'clock in the morning, there were few travelers in the airport terminal lobby. Except for the piped-in soft jazz music playing in the background, it was eerily quiet. Morrie's duffel bag was a carry-on, so he had no need to stop at the luggage carousel, but made straight for the doors providing exit to the parking area. He stepped outside and instinctively shivered in the near-freezing temperature; the sun's rays had not yet burned through the overcasting cloud and fog bank.

Glad I left my warm parka in my car, Morrie thought. His eyes surveyed the sparsely filled lot, searching for sight of his forest green MG. The total of vehicles parked in the airport lot were readily visible from where he stood. *I can't believe she'd forget...running late, I guess...although she is used to being at work in the Emporium by eight in the morning.*

Morrie paced rapidly back and forth, trying to stay as warm as possible in his lightweight corduroy blazer, while he awaited Pei's arrival with his winter jacket. Fifteen minutes elapsed. *Better give her a call...if she's not still there, Ben can tell me how long ago she left to pick me up.* He punched numbers on his cell phone and heard the ringing. He let it ring a dozen times; no one answered.

She must be on her way...but where is Ben at this early hour? Maybe he's downstairs, preparing the Emporium for re-opening. Morrie returned inside the terminal and strode to the snack bar. *I'll get something hot to sip while I wait.*

Outdoors again, Morrie stood gulping hot chocolate and scanning the landscape for sight of his sportcar. He drained the Styrofoam cup, crumpled it in his hand and tossed it into a nearby trash receptacle. He tried calling the Wu apartment again; there was no response to repeated ringing. He glanced at his wristwatch. *I've been waiting almost an hour! Where could she be?* Worst-case scenarios kaleidoscoped through his imagination; concern for Pei was equal to his anxiety about his beloved vintage automobile.

A yellow sedan stopped in front of him, its engine idling. "Taxi?" The driver leaned across the front seat of his cab and addressed Morrie.

"Yes." Morrie disconnected the 'phone call and slipped the gadget into the inside pocket of his blazer. He grabbed his duffel bag, hopped into the back seat of the taxi and told the driver his home address; the cab lurched forward. Through the rear window, Morrie continued to watch for the overdue arrival of his sportcar, until the cab merged with the flow of traffic on the street.

Between vinyl-coated wires of his enclosure, Fair Rhett peered up at Morrie. *I've never seen such a sad expression on his face... He's knocked over his food bowl!... Never done that before.*

Morrie shut the door to his apartment, dropped his duffel and immediately knelt to unlatch the habitat gate. The ferret leaped into Morrie's outstretched hands. *He's lost weight! No food in the cage...when was Pei here last?...contents of the litter box scattered, and the waste hasn't been removed lately!*

"Poor F'Rhett!" Morrie held the joyfully chortling ferret against his chest and petted him, carrying him into the kitchenette. With one hand, he extracted an opened can of kitten food from the refrigerator, sniffed it, discarded it, and pulled an unopened can of kitten food from a cupboard. He placed the ferret on a chair from which he could watch Morrie open the can and scoop a teaspoonful onto a clean saucer. *I wonder how long it's been since he last ate...don't want to make him sick by giving him too much too soon.* He set the saucer of food on the floor; Fair Rhett gobbled it and looked up expectantly at Morrie.

"Second helping in a few minutes, after that morsel settles," Morrie promised, crossing the apartment to check the water level in his pet's feeder bottle. The animal scampered close by Morrie's heels.

"Uh-huh, thought so," He detached the bottled and refilled it from the jug of pure, spring water that was the source of Morrie's own drinking water.

Morrie tossed a rattle-toy onto the carpet; Fair Rhett glanced at it, but returned to the kitchenette and stood next to the refrigerator.

"Okay," Morrie sighed and spooned more moist kitten food onto Fair Rhett's saucer. While the ferret dined, Morrie thoroughly cleaned the animal's habitat, washed the litter box and refilled it with new, pine-scented pellets.

Now, the 'phone calls. He pressed the button to hear accumulated messages:

"Morrie, what's awl this I hear about you and Tofu? Would it kill you to cawl and let me know what's happening, once in awhile?" The exasperated voice was his mother's.

The tape rolled on: "Mr. Maccabbee, this is Sergeant Pillsbury at police headquarters. Please give me a call back at your earliest convenience."

What could that be about? Morrie frowned. *First, have to find Pei and my car.* On his wall telephone, he pressed the familiar sequence of numbers and listened to the ringing continue uninterrupted by anyone at the Wu residence. *Maybe they are both downstairs getting the market ready for* business...that's why she forgot to pick me up this morning. His fingers danced upon another series of numbers and he listened to more ringing. *Nobody at the Emporium, either.* He sighed, disconnected the sound and returned one of the messaged calls.

"Police headquarters, Officer Stanley speaking," a female voice answered.

"This is Morrie Maccabbee, returning a call from Sergeant Pillsbury."

"Sergeant Pillsbury is not in today. What was the call in reference to?"

"I don't know. I'm just returning his call."

"Sergeant Pillsbury will be here Monday; you may contact him then."

"Okay. Thanks. Goodbye."

Monday! That's four days...maybe Officer Miller knows why the department called me...maybe I can still catch him and Smith at their morning break. A glimpse of the time revealed that he had ten minutes to get to the bus stop.

He hesitated briefly; watching Fair Rhett's rambunctious, happy dancing from one side of the flat to the other, Morrie was reluctant to confine him again so soon. *If I leave him out, running like crazy through the apartment, he's apt to do something silly and hurt himself.* He scratched the top of the ferret's head and placed him, along with a few kibbles in a clean play-sock, into the habitat. *That'll keep him busy for a little while, I hope.*

Morrie pulled his old, brown leather, bomber-pilot-style jacket from his closet, gathered his keys and dashed to catch a public transit bus that would promptly deliver him downtown.

I'm in luck! Morrie saw the marked squad car parked, as usual, in the no parking zone directly in front of The Cuppa Cabana.

Sweet blueberry and vanilla flavors, exuding from a tray of bouffant muffins just removed from the oven, perfumed the air that wafted past Morrie as he entered the popular cafe.

"Morrie, good to see you!" Cora, the smiling waitress exclaimed. Officers Van Miller and Chuck Smith slightly pivoted their counter stools to acknowledge Morrie's entrance. He took a seat two stools down the counter from the pair of men in blue uniforms. Cora's brown hands placed a steaming cup of the restaurant's famous coffee before him.

"How about a fresh blueberry muffin to go with your cuppa?" she cordially inquired.

"You read my mind!" Morrie told her, his cold hands juggling for a warm position around the mug of coffee.

"I don't see your hot rod," Officer Miller said. "Thought you'd have collected it by now."

"'Collected it'? You know where my car is?" Morrie asked.

The officers exchanged questioning glances.

"Didn't Pillsbury call you?" Miller queried.

"He left a message on my answering machine. I've been out of town all week." Morrie took a sip of coffee before continuing. "When I called back, about half an hour ago, I was told he wasn't there today. He called about my car?"

"Yeah," Officer Smith too solemnly replied.

"Was it in an accident?" Morrie leaped from his seat. "What about the driver?" His heart missed a beat.

"No, no. Relax," Miller said.

Morrie's knees bent again and he sat back upon the counter stool.

"Your vehicle looked just fine, as far as I could tell," Miller assured. "Smith and I happened to be crossing the impound lot a couple of days ago and were surprised to see what we were pretty sure was your little old MG there."

"We checked with the officer on duty, who happened to be Pillsbury," Smith related. "He confirmed that it was registered in your name."

"Pillsbury said he'd called you immediately, as soon as it was towed in," Miller added.

"Towed in!" Morrie was appalled; his neglected muffin was cold.

"Well, yeah," Miller responded. "You'll have to get the details from the arresting officer's report."

"What about the wom -- the person who was driving my car?" Morrie inquired.

"Never occurred to us that anyone but you would have been driving your MG," Smith muttered, not quite suppressing the smirk that struggled to express his response to Morrie's revelation that he had allowed a female to drive his precious antique.

"Don't know anything about whoever was driving, if it wasn't you," Miller concurred and gulped the last of his coffee.

"You'll have to get details from the apprehending officer's report," Smith repeated Miller's advice.

"She's missing, too," Morrie admitted, disappointed that Miller or Smith knew nothing about her whereabouts.

The officers exchanged expressions of thinly veiled bemusement.

"Little wonder," Smith said. "If I was stopped for a traffic violation while driving your MG, I just might go missing, too!"

"Pillsbury thought the vehicle might have been stolen," Miller said.

"Well, then, if she was arrested, she might still be in jail," Morrie realized.

"Unless somebody bailed her out," Smith suggested.

Officer Miller arose from his seat and stepped to stand next to Morrie.

"Come on, we'll give you a lift to the station. You can redeem your wheels and read the officer's citation."

The three men left currency on the counter for Cora to collect when she wasn't busy with other customers, and exited the Cuppa Cabana.

"So your car wasn't stolen; the person driving it had your permission?" The uniformed young woman at the police station tossed her pony-tailed head and looked expectantly at Morrie through the transparent pane that, as a precautionary measure, separated department staff from visitors. She wanted confirmation that she had correctly summarized his story.

"Absolutely! What, exactly, is she charged with?" Morrie asked.

"I'll have to pull that information. Just give me a minute, here," she said, poking computer keys.

"Here we are...Megler Street, just past 10th Avenue...failure to stop before entering intersection."

"I know that corner! Tree leaves conceal the stop sign; if you don't know it's there, you're likely to miss it!" Morrie protested.

"It's February," the officer calmly reminded Morrie, turning to fully face him. "The branches are bare, there are no leaves to obstruct visibility."

"Is that all? May I just pay the fine and get my vehicle and my friend released?" Morrie sighed his exasperation.

"No, there's more," the officer said, returning her attention to the computer screen.

"Showing disrespect for an officer...rude demeanor," she read.

"What? Not Pei; she's a quiet, reserved, extremely polite lady," Morrie insisted. "She couldn't be disrespectful if she tried; honor is in her blood, it's her heritage!"

"When he asked to see her driver license, she laughed at him," the officer informed.

Morrie shook his head in disbelief.

"And when he asked her to show him some other form of identification, because she didn't have a driver license, she laughed again," the officer continued reading.

Morrie suddenly remembered Pei's self-conscious giggle and knew what had happened when the imposing authority had questioned her, misunderstood her habitual, albeit objectionable, response.

"She was nervous and frightened," Morrie explained. "Oriental people sometimes express those emotions by giggling. She wasn't being intentionally rude."

"Yeah, right," the officer smirked.

"Really. I've read about how, during World War II, captured Japanese soldiers responded to interrogation with giggles," Morrie informed. "That irritated and confused our troops until they learned that is an autonomous nervous system stress response for Orientals."

"Uh-huh." She didn't believe him, and continued reading: "Driving without license...failure to provide any means of identification..." Her brows puckered, then raised before she uttered "Uh-oh."

"I can release your vehicle to you, but I am unable to help you with your friend," she said, turning to accept the bank check Morrie was filling-out to cover impound fees.

"Why not?" Morrie stared at her.

"I'm sorry, but you'll have to speak with Sergeant Pillsbury about that, and he is not on duty today," she apologized. "You may reach him here on Monday."

Morrie inhaled audibly and pushed the payment through the slot in the separating pane.

"May I at least see Pei?" he asked.

The officer hesitated, then gently replied: "I'm sorry, that's not possible. She isn't here."

"Not here? Then where is she? Has she been released on her own recognizance?" Morrie demanded.

"I can't tell you any more because you are not a member of her immediate family." Her eyes would not meet Morrie's. "Here is the receipt you need to show to the attendant who will release your car to you. Have a nice day."

Standing at the top of the iron staircase, Morrie had no more begun to rap his knuckles against the door to the Wu flat before Ben Wu pulled the door open.

"Ah, gummy-shoe. Please come in. Good to see you."

Morrie entered the apartment and seated himself on the familiar worn sofa to which his host gestured.

"Is Pei here?" Morrie immediately broached the reason for his visit.

"No! Not here since Tuesday!" Ben revealed, seating himself in an upholstered arm-chair. "She go to tend your animal Monday morning, Monday evening, Tuesday morning, Tuesday evening, but not come home again."

"Did you file a missing person report with the police?" Morrie asked.

"Cannot do that." Ben's reply was soft and low.

"Why not? Aren't you worried about her?"

"Very, very worried."

"Well, then?" Morrie pressed.

"They would find out Pei is not legal resident in this country; no social security number, no green card."

"And, consequently, no driver license," A low whistle escaped Morrie's lips. "But she made deliveries in your van!"

Ben's shoulders shrugged.

"So you would be in big trouble, too, with government authorities, because you employed her," Morrie commented.

Ben nodded his affirmation of Morrie's statement, and added: "Harboring alien not good, either. I make tea," Ben said, starting to rise from his chair.

"No, thank you. Please don't bother. I can't stay." Morrie refrained from adding that he was eager to return home and spend some time with Fair Rhett, to try and make-up for the attention he had been deprived of over the last two and a half days.

Ben repeated his head-nod and resettled into his chair.

"How do you intend to find Pei, without help from the police?" Morrie inquired.

"Ask gummy-shoe!" Ben brightened. "That's what you do, yes? Find people?"

"Mostly cats," Morrie muttered. "Of course I'll be trying to find her."

Morrie arose and walked to the door; Ben followed and opened it for him.

"I'll let you know as soon as I find her; and you let me know immediately if you hear from her, please." Morrie stepped outside. "No matter what time of day or night that might be."

Ben nodded again and somberly closed the door.

No need to contribute to Ben's worries by telling him that Pei was stopped by a traffic cop. He'd be apprehensive that Pei's trail would lead the authorities directly to him, that they'd be knocking on his door any minute...as well they might.

❦

"You are a natural dancer," Morrie told Kim as they crossed the gymnasium parking lot after folk dancing. "And your new friends are a fringe benefit!"

That Kim's handsome features, quiet charm and courteousness plus his agility and talent on the dance floor made the young man a chick-magnet had not gone unnoticed by Morrie.

"It's fun. I'll go whenever you can pick me up," the lanky lad replied.

"You're on for every Friday!" Morrie assured him, reversing his MG from the parking slot and steering it through a snappy turn.

"Thank you. I'll be there on the C.C.I. steps by six-thirty every Friday," Kim's tone brimmed with enthusiasm.

"You know, I could just as easily pick you up at your home, if you'll tell me where that is," Morrie urged.

"Maybe later. Just not a good idea right now," Kim replied, preferring not to reveal his reason: the vintage roadster would undoubtedly be noticed in his neighborhood -- it always drew attention, wherever it went -- and Kim did not want his current pals to recognize any clues to the fact that he was making some positive changes in his activities and associations.

"I see the photograph of Madame Wu is still on display in the window," Morrie observed when they rolled past the Oriental Imports Emporium. "How long is the mourning period, do you know?"

"Usually 30 days, I think," Kim murmured; he gazed forward, not turning his head toward the market.

"The robber who cleaned out the cash register and killed her still has not been apprehended," Morrie commented. "At least, I've not read that there's been any arrest made in the case."

Morrie signaled and eased the roadster into the left lane, continuing: "The guy must have been desperate, to commit a brutal crime like that for the few bucks in the register."

"It was an accident!" Kim blurted.

"Wha-at?" Morrie instinctively braked, as if slowing their movement would, somehow, make Kim's words more comprehensible.

"What do you know about it?" Morrie demanded.

"Nothing! I didn't say that!"

Taking advantage of the car's reduced speed, Kim leaped from the coupe and dashed, amidst honking horns and squealing brakes, across the right-hand lane of oncoming traffic to the sidewalk.

"Holy shit!" Morrie muttered.

Unable to veer right and penetrate traffic, wanting to park at the curb and give chase on foot, Morrie observed Kim sprinting around the next corner and down a side street. Morrie cruised across the intersection and was then able to access the right lane. He curved the sportcar's track around the second corner and made another right turn, attempting to regain sight of Kim.

That didn't happen.

SATURDAY 2

Lama Trisong directed me to Dancing Dragon for some good reason, I'm sure, was Morrie's first thought upon awakening; *and I didn't discover that reason when I visited the gallery last week. I'll drop in again today...this afternoon.*

Fair Rhett pawed at the latch on his habitat. Morrie arose and freed the furry mammal, who charged the futon, scrambling among the bedding as his master gathered and folded it for daytime storage in a lidded wicker basket on a bookshelf.

In the kitchenette of his compact studio apartment, Morrie discovered he was out of his breakfast staple, English muffins. *Should have gone grocery shopping yesterday...* Opening the door to the freezer compartment of his refrigerator, he spied an alternative: "Ah, an apple turnover."

Behind him, out of Morrie's sight, Fair Rhett suddenly lay flat and rolled over.

The wall telephone rang; Morrie reached to grab the receiver. "Maccabbee here."

"Hey, Morrie, if you've got a minute or two, I'd like to hear how you and Kim are getting along. How'd it go last night?"

145

"Sure, Mike. Just give me a second to put an apple turnover in the micro."

This time, when the ferret rolled, Morrie happened to be watching. *Weird! He's never done that before.*

Morrie's brow puckered in puzzlement. He continued to observe the animal's activity during the conversation with his tennis buddy, Mike, who earned his living as a social worker, a youth counselor.

"Okay, I'm back," Morrie spoke into the mouthpiece. "Kim's picking up advanced footwork patterns already; and we're getting along just fine. Nice kid."

"That will go a long way toward helping separate him from the hoodlums he was running around with. You think he'll stick with it? What is the folk dance attrition rate, anyway?" Mike asked.

"I'll take him with me every Friday," Morrie said, his eyes still focused on his pet. "As for drop-outs, well, if someone attends for three consecutive sessions, they're usually hooked. It's a low rate of turn-over."

Fair Rhett stretched, rolled and stared expectantly at Morrie.

"That's reassuring. I sure appreciate -- "

"Mike, may I call you back later? Fair Rhett is doing something peculiar. I need to look into it."

"He's not sick is he?" Mike was concerned.

"No, no. He's just doing something he never did before."

"Okay, later." Mike disconnected.

With a raisin pinched between two fingers, Morrie squatted next to the ferret.

"Turn over, F'Rhett," he ordered.

The ferret did as he was told. Morrie stroked the top of his pet's head and fed him the raisin.

"I never taught you that trick! Where did you learn to do that, you little rascal?" *Pei must have taught him, earlier this week.*

After breakfasting and dressing, Morrie sorted the mail that had been delivered during his absence the last few days. Most items were dropped, unopened, directly into a wastebasket. But there was the current issue of Foster & Smith ferret catalogue and a personal letter. Morrie glanced at the return address. *From Judy Rosen...why didn't she just call, or email, if she had something to tell me?*

He slit the envelope; a bank check fell out onto his desk. He extracted the accompanying handwritten note from his mother's neighbor and long-time family friend:

> Morrie, dear:
>
> Mickey saw you carrying precious Tofu across our backyard Friday, just seconds before he reappeared indoors. Thank you!
>
> Love, Judy

As the previous Saturday, the Dancing Dragon Asian Art Gallery was devoid of customers when Morrie stepped across the threshold onto its dense, wall-to-wall carpeting. The door to Auden Lewellyn's private office was closed; but, although words were not clearly audible, Morrie heard voices behind it.

Morrie stood admiring a display of ceremonial axes, many dating as far back as 400 B.C. Some were of intricately carved jade, others were highly decorated cast bronze; some adorned with human or animal figures. He was studying the geometric designs and stylized dragon relief on the largest artifact -- a carved, dark green jade axe nearly three feet in length, with sharply pointed spear at one end and a circular loop for hanging at the opposite end -- when the proprietor's office door opened and two teenage Chinese males exited.

"Too bad about the old lady. She shouldn't have tried to interfere." Lewellyn's voice and personage followed the boys.

If they noticed Morrie, the boys didn't acknowledge his presence, but rapidly crossed the showroom and left the building via the main entrance. Seeing Morrie, Lewellyn's steps stopped abruptly; he frowned.

"Ah, Mr. Maccabbee. Have you decided to become an art collector, after all?" Auden Lewellyn feigned cordiality.

"No. I don't have enough space in my apartment to allow me to collect anything but dust," Morrie replied. Lewellyn's parting words to the Chinese teenagers echoed in Morrie's conscience. The man's pale grey eyes stared questioningly at him.

"I dropped in to ask if you have seen Pei Jiangiyn lately," Morrie explained.

"Who is Pei Jiangiyn?" Lewellyn inquired; his frown persisted.

"The young lady who worked at the Emporium," Morrie reminded. "She's been missing since Tuesday."

"Oh. No. Not since our meeting in the restaurant in Castlevale," Lewellyn replied. "What is your occupation, Mr. Maccabbee? May I receive the courtesy of your business card?"

From his wallet, Morrie withdrew one of his cards and handed it to Lewellyn, who perused the imprint and remarked:

"I see. And today you are investigating what?"

"Pei's disappearance," Morrie replied calmly.

"And perhaps more." Lewellyn pulled a cell phone from the breast pocket of his tweed sport coat and punched seven buttons.

"Such as?" Morrie prompted.

"You were here a week ago, obviously not shopping. That was three days before the young woman disappeared, you say; so you were clearly not investigating her absence then." Lewellyn stepped back away from Morrie and spoke into his 'phone, his tone low:

"Bao, please return to the gallery. I need you." Lewellyn paused to listen, then spoke again into the 'phone: "I know that, but there has been an unexpected development here that requires your assistance to resolve. Immediately, thank you."

The importer slipped the 'phone back into his coat pocket and faced Morrie, stating frankly:

"I think you overheard some of my conversation with the boys a few minutes ago. I have noticed your frequent visits to Ben Wu's residence. Now that I know you are a private investigator, it is a ready conclusion that Mr. Wu, understandably discouraged by the police investigation which has turned up nothing of significance, has hired you to work on the case of his wife's murder."

As Lewellyn spoke, Morrie, sensing danger, inched backward toward the exit.

"You are wrong. Mr. Wu has not hired me to find his wife's killer," Morrie informed. "He has, however, asked me to locate Pei, but that is something I am doing for my own personal reasons." He turned and bolted for the door just as Bao, ubiquitous cigarette unlit between his lips, entered, blocking the doorway.

"Shut the door, Bao," Lewellyn ordered. "Mr. Maccabbee is not leaving."

Intending to wedge himself through the narrow opening between Bao and the door frame, Morrie thrust his weight forward. There was no way he could have known that Bao was in his tenth year of martial arts practice.

Auden Lewellyn retrieved Morrie's eyeglasses and cap from their surprise landing on the carpet. Bao firmly held Morrie's arms twisted tightly against the sleuth's back.

"You will not be needing these again," the importer declared, setting Morrie's glasses and hat atop a display case.

"There are people who know of my plans to visit Dancing Dragon this afternoon," Morrie warned, wholly regretting that his statement was not true.

"Nor will you need these," Lewellyn said, frisking Morrie and taking his cell phone, keys, wallet and pocket tape recorder. "Is this turned on? No? You are slipping, Mr. Private Eye."

"Private eye? Is that what this guy is?" Bao asked, gazing at Morrie with unconcealed admiration.

"He is -- or was -- on the trail of Madame Wu's killer," Lewellyn informed Bao; the latter's expression changed abruptly and he looked to Auden Lewellyn to dictate the next move.

"Take him downstairs," the importer commanded, leading the way to a door next to his private office. "Bind his wrists with some of that cord used to reinforce large shipping cartons," Lewellyn continued, opening the door to reveal a steep stairwell. His thumb jabbed a light-switch, illuminating but dimly the cellar. "Use some packing material to gag him."

"Oh, man! I'm no good at knots!" Bao protested. "Need Kim's fingers for that kind of job!"

"That may well be," the importer responded, "but, in case you haven't noticed, your friend is not present here at this moment in time."

Bao shoved Morrie, who resisted every step, down the narrow stairwell; his last-ditch effort to free himself gained him only more gratuitous pain.

At the foot of the stairs, the first thing Bao did was light his cigarette as soon as the door at the top of the steps was closed.

While Bao mumbled, hummed, dragged on his cigarette and simultaneously wrapped Morrie's wrists, Morrie's eyes surveyed -- as well as they could without prescription lenses -- that portion of the cellar that was visible, albeit dimly so, in front and to the sides of him.

A few crates of varied dimensions were stacked against a wall; upon them lay plastic bubble-wrap, segments of twine and sheets of wrapping paper. *There's probably a knife, too, among that stuff...or scissors,* Morrie told himself.

The door at the top of the stairs opened a few inches.

"What's taking you so long, Bao?" Lewellyn called. "Put out that cigarette!"

Bao cursed, dropped the cigarette and, with one booted foot, crushed it into the ground.

"He hates smoke," Bao said apologetically, as if he owed Morrie an explanation. He tested his knots, grunted in satisfaction and returned back up the stairs.

"What are we gonna do with him now?" Bao's voice was audible through the floorboards above Morrie.

"Antonio owes me a big favor," Lewellyn replied. "I'm calling it in."

"Will you need me Monday morning to load the shipment?" Bao asked.

"No, thank you. The freight-truck driver can handle it this time."

"Is that detective gonna be out of here by then?" Bao was apprehensive.

"I shall call Antonio as soon as I arrive home. He will be apprised of the urgency of the situation and I'm certain he will have one of his men over here before morning to take care of our guest."

Bao lingered only long enough to accept a wad of currency from Lewellyn.

Morrie felt the vibration from Lewellyn's heavy footsteps overhead and heard the slap of a bolt sliding into place, securing the door to the cellar. The light vanished. It was as dank and dark as a dungeon.

SUNDAY 2

Lama Jigme Trisong Rinpoche stood, steaming tea bowl in both hands, gazing through his window at a snow-blanketed landscape; the glistening whiteness illuminated the night.

Awaken to lovely surprise...only an inch or so, but it is beautiful. The smiling lama's eyes sparkled with delight to view the crystalline scene -- until his keen sight captured the silhouette of a familiar roadster parked across the street from the Dancing Dragon Asian Art Gallery. *Exactly where it was when I retired yesterday;* a frown replaced his smile.

He rinsed his tea bowl, dried it meticulously with a towel and returned it to its resting place on the teakwood storage chest. *Dancing Dragon closed on Sunday and Monday...why Mr. Maccabee's car still there, not moved...unless...nothing good or bad, everything just is...no, this is bad.*

He removed his red wool greatcoat from a wall hook and draped it across his shoulders, stepped out of his room, padded down the stairs quietly to avoid disturbing the sleep of his landlord, the martial arts master, at this pre-dawn hour, and departed the building via the rear exit.

Might wake the old man, too, but that cannot be helped.

155

An awkward feel-about in complete darkness among packing material for a sharp blade to sever the cord that bound his hands had not been necessary for Morrie. Boa's clumsy fingers, Auden Lewellyn's demand to hurry, plus the diameter and texture of the rope all totaled a knot that loosened after but a few minutes of wrestling with it.

When the street lamp came on, a horizontal strip of pale light delineated the bottom edge of a door that Morrie had not noticed earlier, when the cellar was illuminated, because it was located in the wall behind him. Now, he felt along the vertical edges of the door to locate hinges, but found none. *Must be on the outside...can't get to them to remove the pins.* His hand found the knob; repeatedly, he turned and pushed to no avail. *It opens out, so...* He tried kicking it open, but his soft leather loafers were not adequate for the job, nor was his 160-pound body, thrust, shoulder leading, against the door.

He had already performed this routine at the top of the stairs, after cautiously feeling his way up the flight of steps to challenge that securely bolted door.

Bao had forgotten to gag him, but Morrie's shouts for help were unheard. *Nobody is going to be in Chinatown's retail district on a Saturday night,* he knew. *If Lewellyn's buddy Antonio sends just one guy maybe I can charge past him... I hope that Antonio isn't the same person as the local mob leader known by that name.*

It was the longest and coldest night of Morrie's life; and it ended when, moments before daybreak, the cellar door creaked open a few inches. Morrie's heart seemed to leap into his throat, its beat accentuating and accelerating. He stepped swiftly toward the door, an elbow posed to jab someone's jugular, a knee readied to simultaneously make violent groin contact with the same party. His fists, his entire body, tensed with anticipation.

No one entered. His ears strained to hear evidence of a presence. He rushed the door and found no one on the other side of it.

Light cast from a nearby street lamp flooded the doorway, illuminating a portion of the cellar. Morrie stepped across the threshold into the alley and turned back to re-close the cellar door, lest his escape be evident. In so doing, he caught a glimpse of something very familiar. He gasped, turned away and hastened down the alley. Though his vision was impaired by the absence of his prescription-lensed spectacles, he perceived foot-gear tracks in the white, powdery snow. *Imprints almost as large as my own shoe size...textured pattern, like the sole of a running shoe,* he observed, keeping pace with the phantom stride.

Intending to use the extra ignition key stored in the jockey-box, Morrie was astonished, when he opened the unlocked passenger door, to discover his chain of keys, wallet, cell 'phone, mini tape recorder, eye glasses and driver cap awaiting on the seat.

Arriving home, Morrie detoured only to release the latch on Fair Rhett's habitat and headed for the shower, shedding the clothes he was wearing as he went. *Hot water and soapy lather never felt so good...thank God for hot water on tap!* As his frigid extremities thawed, and his mind revived, the urgency of all that he had to do took precedence in his overloaded mind. By the time he was dressed in clean blue jeans and an old, favorite burgundy cashmere pullover sweater, he had prioritized a to-do list.

Because he had not eaten since his breakfast the previous day, number one on the list was food. He blended ingredients for a power beverage and shared that with Fair Rhett. *Planned to go grocery shopping last night...no muffins this morning, either.* He toasted an apple turnover; when he had eaten most of it, he stooped to give his pet a command: "Turn over!"

The ferret did as he was told and was rewarded with a pinch of fruit from the apple turnover.

Morrie tried to avoid thoughts of Pei. *Don't think about the pink elephant in the parlor!* He quipped to himself.

Two 'phone calls were next on his list; he made the first contact.

"Hello?" Ben Wu responded.

"Morrie Maccabbee here, Ben,"

"Ah, gummy-shoe! What do you know?"

"Maybe something that will surprise you," Morrie replied. "I want you to go downstairs and see if your marble statue of Quan Yin riding an elephant is still in your curio cabinet."

"'Course it is!" Ben exclaimed.

"Are you certain? When did you last see it there?"

"Ahh..." Ben hesitated.

"Not since the, uh, not since you closed the Emporium, right?"

"No. Not go down there. Ghost of Ma down there."

"How much money do you suppose that figurine is worth, in today's dollars?" Morrie inquired.

"Oh, pro'ly twenty thousand, more, less."

"Which do you fear more, the ghost of Ma or the loss of that statuette?"

"Ah..." Ben's thoughts vacillated.

"Ben, I think I know where that artifact is, but I need you to confirm that it is missing from your possession."

"You see it somewhere else?" Ben was aghast.

"I think so."

"Where?" Ben demanded.

"I'll tell you that as soon as you tell me whether yours is gone. Please go downstairs and take a look."

"Ah..." Ben's breathing was audible. "Okay. Be right back. Just put 'phone down right here. Don't hang up, okay?"

"No, I'll hold the line," Morrie assured him.

Morrie heard the door to the Wu flat close; a minute later he heard it slam, then Ben's voice:

"It's gone! Big statue of Quan Yin on elephant is gone! Very rare, very valuable!"

"Yeah, that's why it's gone," Morrie wryly remarked. "It's in the cellar at Dancing Dragon Asian Art Gallery."

"No! How it get there?"

"It's what the burglar was really after, not merely cash from the register," Morrie told him. "Do you have some kind of documentation that will prove provenance, prove your ownership of that statuette?"

"Dunno. Had it for a long time...see what I can find. Maybe picture, too?"

"That will help. And I can testify that I saw it many times in the Emporium," Morrie promised.

"How we get it back?"

"I'm working on that."

"Gummy-shoe, you get Quan Yin back and find Pei, I give you Quan Yin statue," Ben declared.

"Oh, Ben, you won't owe me -- REALLY?"

Morrie's next call was to his long-time friend and tennis buddy, Mike Lerner, who was also Kim's counselor.

"Hey, Morrie!" Mike's bass voice boomed. "What's happening?"

"How about, I just escaped from captivity in a cold, damp cellar," Morrie retorted.

"Yeah? Well, whatever," Mike cajoled.

"And it was Kim who opened the door so I could get out."

"Kim? Our young dancer?"

"Yes. And because he probably saved my life, his is now in danger. I need to know where he lives so I can talk with him and get him to safety."

"Oh, wow, Morrie. You know that's classified information. I could lose my job, and any future jobs, as well, if I revealed the address of a client."

"Just how many people do you think I plan to share the information with?" Morrie's sarcasm was thinly veiled.

"Nobody?"

"Absolutely nobody. Well, maybe the police. I won't even write it down, I'll memorize it."

Mike inhaled deeply and exhaled noisily, mulling a decision.

"They killed Madame Wu and have nothing to lose but plenty to gain by getting rid of Kim because he --"

"Just a minute," Mike interrupted.

Fair Rhett tickled Morrie's feet. Morrie lifted the animal onto his lap and stroked the top of his housemate's head.

"12 Locust," Mike read into the 'phone.

"Thank you. I'll get back to you with the details as soon as I have them sorted out," Morrie assured his friend.

"Let me know if, as Kim's case worker, I can help him out of the mess he apparently is in."

"Right. The authorities will be in touch with you, I'm sure." *Like, in about two hours,* Morrie silently added, returning the receiver to its repose.

By mid-morning, all traces of the light snowfall had melted beneath a cloudless blue sky that permitted reprieve from the low temperatures by way of unobstructed sunshine.

Morrie eased his vintage roadster to the Locust Street curb a few houses beyond number twelve. He punched a familiar sequence of numbers into his cell phone and conversed briefly with parties at the receiving end of the call before stepping out of the vehicle.

He strode past the row of identical, tiny homes, the first residences constructed in Chinatown. Aging now, all were in need of major repair of one kind or another; neglect was evident. Squinting against the brilliant sunlight, Morrie turned from the sidewalk to rap his knuckles upon the door of house number twelve. A window curtain ruffled slightly; Morrie was aware that someone was looking to see who was at their door.

The door was opened only a crack.

"How did you know where to find me?" Kim's widened, sleepy eyes bespoke his surprise.

"A little birdie told me," Morrie utilized the classic 'I'll never tell' answer. "I don't think either of us want me to be seen standing on your doorstep."

"I'm avoiding some people," Kim explained, opening the door just wide enough to admit Morrie.

"No kidding. That's an excellent idea," Morrie said, stepping into the small parlor that was further dwarfed by a six-foot long couch covered by a rumpled sheet and a blanket.

"I sleep here," the boy informed. "My grandfather has the only bedroom." He rolled the bedding into a loose wad against one arm of the worn couch and plopped onto the cleared area.

Morrie seated himself upon the tattered upholstery of an easy chair.

"You unlocked the door to the cellar under Dancing Dragon earlier this morning, didn't you?" Morrie didn't have time to beat-around-the-bush.

"Lama Trisong was here, he told me to," Kim admitted sheepishly.

"Thank you. You probably saved my life, so yours is in jeopardy now, for doing that, you know."

Kim nodded; his eyes expressed fear.

"Tell me all you know about Madame Wu's murder, so I can give the authorities good reason to protect you," Morrie ordered.

Kim's tongue slid slowly over his lips; his gaze focused down upon a stain on the hardwood floor.

Behind Morrie, a figure parted the curtains hanging in the entrance to the kitchen and stood on the threshold.

"I...I don't know anything," the fearful lad muttered.

"Kim, I saw you," the figure framed by the doorway spoke softly.

Morrie's head turned to see who had spoken. *That's Shin Lam!*

"This is my grandfather," Kim said to Morrie; then to the old man: "I am sorry you have been disturbed again."

"I saw you," Shin Lam repeated; "Saw you leaving the Emporium with two other boys."

"We don't have much time left," Morrie glanced at his wristwatch. "You have to get out of here, or your grandfather's in danger, too."

"Aiyee!" The old man retreated through the curtains to his bedroom at the rear of the house.

"It was an accident!" Kim insisted.

"All right," Morrie said amiably, placing his left ankle across his bent right knee. "Tell me about it."

"I just picked the lock on the cabinet. Lung took out a big statue of Quan Yin. Bao was standing watch. I was rearranging stuff on the shelf so nobody would notice something was missing, Suddenly, the old lady came in and told us to get out. We started to leave, but when she saw Lung had the statue, she said she was going to call the police. Bao grabbed her, hooked his arm around her neck."

Kim paused in his narration; he was loosing the battle opposing his tears. His eyes brimmed and his voice cracked.

"Go on," Morrie encouraged, adjusting his parka.

"He didn't mean to kill her! He didn't know how frail she was, that her neck bones were so -- so old," Kim sobbed.

"Osteoporosis," Morrie gently informed him. "Our bones lose density with age, becoming thin and vulnerable."

"Bao is very strong, He doesn't know his strength, sometimes," Kim sniffled. "Lung said we should take the money from the register to make it look like a hold-up."

"Was Auden Lewellyn with you?" Morrie asked pointedly.

"No. He never goes on the heists," Kim said. "But I'm not working for him anymore, not after that night. I tell them I have homework, my part-time hours at the burger joint, and that I have to care for my grandfather."

"And that is all true," Morrie consoled, casually reaching into a pocket of his parka to depress the off button on his concealed tape-recorder.

Through the sheer curtains covering the parlor window that faced Locust Street, Morrie observed an unmarked police car come to a halt in front of Shin Lam's house.

"Your testimony is valuable; you can plea bargain. You'll have to spend some time in juvenile detention, for your safety. Mike -- er, Mr. Lerner will help you. If he's not at the station when you get there, he soon will be." Morrie rose, looked intently at Kim's red-rimmed eyes and tear-stained, distressed countenance and added, "Wipe your face."

Out front, two officers in plain clothes erupted from the squad car.

Kim leaned sideways to reach the balled sheet and swiped an edge of it across his face. Morrie offered him a high-five; the sorry lad solemnly slapped his palm against Morrie's.

The fateful sound of rapidly approaching footsteps was followed immediately by a puissant knocking against the front door.

"Police! Open up!"

MONDAY 3

The sting occurred just before daybreak.

Lama Trisong, from his chilly room above the martial arts studio, bowl of warming tea in hand, observed the arrival of a sport utility van on Pine Street; it came to a stop at the curb several yards from the Dancing Dragon Asian Art Gallery.

Four men in flak jackets slipped out of the vehicle. Their weapons concealed, Lama Trisong could not know they were armed. One pair walked swiftly to the main entrance of the gallery, out of the lama's sight. The remaining two men advanced with lengthy strides up the alley to assume positions by the gallery's cellar door, one at each side. Auden Lewellyn's sedan was present in the alley.

As soon as the gallery proprietor, attempting to evade the Federal Bureau of Investigation agents at his front door, burst out of the cellar exit, the two waiting agents promptly encircled his wrists with steel cuffs. The other pair of special agents soon emerged from the cellar, carrying crates readied for shipment.

"Ahh..." sighed the lama. He swallowed the last of his morning beverage, stepped away from the window, rinsed the tea bowl and pot, and settled onto his floor mat facing the colorful illustration of Buddha for his long meditation period.

At some point during his enforced, short march from Dancing Dragon to the SUV, Auden Lewellyn realized that the house in Castlevale had been a set-up.

Federal authorities had Lewellyn's activities under surveillance for only a few weeks before items they knew, by tracking his website solicitations, were on his want list came into FBI possession when a number of stolen antiquities was confiscated during an unrelated raid.

When an FBI agent offered the temporary use of an unoccupied rental property in Castlevale, the three carved jade columns that had been stolen from a Neolithic royal tomb were marked for later identification and placed on display in the house. Eastern antiquities specialist Auden Lewellyn was contacted by a special agent representing herself as the homeowner and art collector desirous of learning the value of those specific pieces.

The trap was set -- and snapped.

As expected, Sergeant Pillsbury, a heavy-set, balding, career officer nearing retirement age, was on duty when Morrie arrived at police headquarters.

"I want to file charges of kidnapping, harassment and suspicion of trafficking in stolen art antiquities," Morrie declared.

"Sure," the burly sergeant said, reaching for the appropriate form and a ballpoint pen. "Your name?"

Morrie provided the statistics required and related details of his captivity; the officer penned in the blanks.

"Kidnapping...first or second degree?" Pillsbury pondered. "Well, I can look up that later. Where did all this happen? Can you give me some names?"

"At the Dancing Dragon Asian Art Gallery. Auden Lewellyn is the proprietor and a kid named --"

"Just a minute, please." Pillsbury turned from Morrie to speak into an intercom system: "Where was the call to assist earlier this morning?" A pause while he listened. "That's what I thought; a name like that, you remember!" He continued to listen to the voice contributing the other half of the dialogue. He cast a quick glance at Morrie, then down at his shoes; he fiddled with the pen, clicking the point back and forth in its cartridge.

"Uh-huh, okay. Thanks." Pillsbury fully returned his attention to Morrie.

"Is there a problem?" Morrie inquired.

"There is for Lewellyn," the sergeant replied. "Special agents took him and some contraband items into FBI custody a few hours ago."

A low whistle escaped Morrie's lips before they curved into a broad smile.

"Their case supercedes anything filed with us," Pillsbury advised.

"Right. But my report can be used to augment the federal suit, can't it?" Morrie suggested.

"Probably. What took you so long to get in here about it?"

"It was more urgent for me to get a young witness into protective custody," Morrie explained, furrowing his brow. "Also, I was told you wouldn't be here until today, and I need to see you about another matter."

Sergeant Pillsbury merely nodded his head and gazed intently at Morrie.

"You left a message on my telephone answering machine last week. I was out of town until Friday," Morrie continued.

The officer referred to a computer and soon told Morrie, "Yes. About your vehicle; but it appears you have picked it up."

"I have. Now, I need to know about the driver. She didn't steal the car; she had my permission to drive it. Where is she? Hasn't she been released yet?"

Pillsbury conferred with the computer again before informing Morrie, "She's not here. ICE was involved. You'll have to contact them."

"Immigration Customs Enforcement!" Morrie exclaimed.

Pillsbury counted off each fact on his fingers as he recited it:

"She couldn't provide any means of identification whatsoever. She was obviously of Oriental ancestry. She was unable to give a local home address. Therefore, she has to be an illegal alien."

Feeling a rare pang of compassion, Officer Pillsbury pulled a fat telephone directory from beneath the counter and perused the federal government listings. Finding the one for which he searched, he scribbled the number on a scratch pad, tore off the page and handed it to Morrie through the slot at the bottom of the pane that separated them.

"Here's the number for ICE. I'm sorry, son, but I don't know anything more than what I've just told you."

"Thanks." Morrie sighed, accepted the slip of paper, pocketed it and exited the police station.

The nearest immigrant detention center is probably in the city...I could be there in four hours or so, Morrie thought, realizing for the first time the depressing possibility that he might never hold Pei in his arms again. *I'll do whatever it takes to prevent her deportation,* he resolved.

Fond memories of Pei occupied his mind during the drive home to his apartment. Almost past a supermarket, he remembered that grocery shopping was long overdue and veered the MG into the strip mall parking lot, anticipating muffins, at last...*turnovers are for clever ferrets!*

❦

"The person you need to speak with will be back about one o'clock," the voice at Immigration Customs Enforcement informed Morrie.

"All right. Thank you. I'll call again this afternoon." Morrie replaced the receiver on his kitchen wall telephone and cast a glance at Fair Rhett, who cocked his head and stared expectantly at his keeper.

"Okay. Lunch." Morrie picked up his housemate and placed him on a dinette chair from which vantage he could watch his meal of scrambled egg being prepared.

Lunch date finished, Morrie decided to pull out all of the ferret's toys from under the hidey-hole beneath his desk and redistribute them around the apartment. Re-gathering them would keep the critter busy while Morrie conversed with ICE.

Lying flat on his stomach, both arms stretched full-length under his desk, Morrie's hands groped for squeaky toys, rattle balls, socks and whatever treasures might comprise the ferret's current cache.

The telephone rang. Several times, in fact, before Morrie could upright himself and leap to grab the receiver,

"Maccabbee here," he spoke breathlessly into the mouthpiece.

"Uh, you okay?"

"Yeh-yeh," Morrie replied; *I can't believe I said that!*

"This is Vince, from folk dancing."

"Sure, Vince. What's happening, man?"

"Our baby girl was born this morning," Vince said proudly.

"Congratulations!"

"Thanks. But it means I have to stay at home with her little big brothers, so I can't pick up the dancer from Scotland when she arrives this evening."

"Say no more, Vince," Morrie assured him. "What's her flight's ETA?"

"Seven-eighteen, but you might want to check on that; winter weather, you know."

"She's probably going to have more luggage than I can stuff into my MG," Morrie advised,

"No doubt. She'll be here for a few months, I understand. She received a grant to research square dancing in its country of origin," Vince told him. "I can go get her gear overflow tomorrow; Laurie's mother will be here then."

"Do we know what she looks like? How will I recognize her?"

"All I know is, she has long, red hair; Scottish, you know. She'll be conducting workshops in Scottish Country Dance for our group, while she's here," Vince said, adding, "Thanks, Morrie."

"Glad to do it, Vince. See you later. Guess I better blow the dust off my ghillies," Morrie quipped.

Noting it was after one o'clock, Morrie punched numbers into his 'phone to connect with the Immigration Customs Enforcement center. His call was promptly transferred to the party with whom he needed to speak.

"This is Mordecai Maccabbee. I am tracing a missing person named Pei Jiangiyn."

"Are you a relative?" the voice, gruff from years of channeling tobacco smoke, routinely asked.

"Yes," Morrie fibbed.

The ICE agent hesitated, pondering how a Maccabbee could possibly be related to a Jiangiyn.

Morrie read his mind and amended his fib:

"I'm her fiancé; we are engaged to be married soon," he embellished.

"Uh-huh. Well, you might want to reconsider the location for your wedding," the rough throat suggested facetiously.

"Why is that?" Morrie frowned.

"Because Pei Jiangiyn will be in Beijing by tomorrow night."

Beijing! Returned to the sickening air pollution that she had forsaken everything to get away from, because her life depended upon living where the atmosphere was salubrious.

"Beijing? Are you certain?" Morrie pressed hopefully.

"I put her on the plane myself, just this morning," the voice confirmed authoritively.

"But it hasn't been a week yet since she was taken into custody," Morrie protested.

"Operation Return to Sender. Too many illegal aliens and not enough facilities to hold them, so the deportation process necessarily has been accelerated," the ICE agent explained.

Morrie groaned his despair.

"In Beijing she'll be transferred to a connecting flight into Ulaanbaatar," the harsh voice continued.

A wave of relief swept through Morrie, slightly easing his regret. *Thank God, she won't be stuck back in Beijing!*

"Yes, she's Mongolian," he mumbled.

"She finally provided us with the name and contact information of her parents in Mongolia. Her father will meet her when her plane lands there."

Smiling now, Morrie concluded the conversation and envisioned details of Pei's homecoming, including the Hotei charm bracelet adorning her left wrist.

I'd better report the news to Ben in person, not over the 'phone, Morrie decided. *I'll stop by on my way to the airport.*

Exhausted from the effort of re-accumulating his belongings, when Morrie placed him into the habitat Fair Rhett immediately retired to his hammock for a long nap.

⚜

Easing his vintage roadster to a stop directly in front of the Oriental Imports Emporium, Morrie noticed the pots of neglected, bedraggled white chrysanthemums and the photograph of Madame Wu had been removed. The interior of the market was fully illuminated. Through the window, glancing over the top of the cafe curtain, he recognized the chubby, muumuu-draped Lily Wang; standing before the antiquated cash register, she was totaling the purchases of a customer.

Morrie strode around a corner of the edifice and down the alley. From the top of the iron staircase came happy Chinese chatter. He looked up to see Ben and Fay Ming descending.

"Ah, gummy-shoe!" Ben called. "You find Pei?"

"Yes," Morrie began; "That is, I found out where she is."

Both Ben and Fay, now standing next to him at the foot of the stairs, stared hopefully at Morrie, who reviewed his conversation with the agent at Immigration Customs Enforcement, concluding:

"And, apparently she never revealed any information about her life here. None of the authorities had any knowledge of her local address."

"She save your bacon!" Fay exclaimed, affectionately focusing her eyes on Ben's placid face.

⚜

At the airport terminal, Morrie paused before pushing the revolving door into the lobby. A rare winter display of hundreds of stars glowing and glittering in the cloudless night sky caught his attention.

I wonder which one is Pei's lucky star. Fervently, he prayed it would continue -- wherever it was -- to shine brilliantly for many decades to come. *But Pei's star would not be visible in this hemisphere,* he remembered, and ceased his appeal to the Western heavens. *I guess it wanted her to come home...maybe it couldn't find her, couldn't guide her, if she stayed here, in this half of the celestial sphere.*

A sudden frigid wind blew against him, caused him to shiver. He turned quickly and pressed his way into the warm lobby. The departures and arrivals board informed that the anticipated flight had landed two minutes ahead of schedule.

Sooner or later, she'll be collecting her luggage, so I might as well wait for her there, Morrie decided.

At the luggage carousel, a young woman with shapely legs extending from beneath a plaid mini-skirt bent forward, reaching for her suitcases. Approaching from behind her, Morrie felt his cheeks flush; he glanced around to see if anyone else had noticed and was glad to see no one else in the immediate area.

The woman straightened and turned to observe the attractive man wearing a tweed driver's cap who sauntered toward her. As he approached her, Morrie's eyes performed a surreptitious once-over of the beautiful lady who, with olive green trench coat folded over one arm, stood before him in the near distance: Navy blue leather pumps; lovely, nylon-stockinged legs; Black Watch woven-wool, mid-thigh-length skirt; green silk ascotted blouse under a navy blue wool blazer; light-catching waves of bright titian hair tousled unrestrained over and past her slim shoulders.

Morrie introduced himself and asked her:

"Has anyone ever told you that your features bear a strong resemblance to those of Botticelli's Venus?"

The sage advises:

Plan to live one hundred years

And to die today.

-- CHINESE PROVERB

LaVergne, TN USA
06 January 2011
211400LV00001B/193/P

9 781589 097407